I0601929

LUNAR BOUND

BOUND TRILOGY INSTALLMENT

GALAXY ALIEN MAIL ORDER BRIDES
BOOK NINE

MICHELLE M. PILLOW

MICHELLEPILLOW.COM

Galaxy Alien Mail Order Brides: Lunar Bound © Copyright 2025, Michelle M. Pillow

First Printing October 14, 2025

Published by The Raven Books LLC

ISBN 978-1-62501-448-1

ALL RIGHTS RESERVED.

This book or any portion thereof may not be reproduced or used in any manner whatsoever without the express written permission of the publisher except for the use of brief quotations in a book review.

This novel is a work of fiction. Any and all characters, events, and places are of the author's imagination and should not be confused with fact. Any resemblance to persons, living or dead, or events or places is merely coincidence.

NO AI TRAINING: Without in any way limiting the author's [and publisher's] exclusive rights under copyright, any use of this publication to "train" generative artificial intelligence (AI) technologies to generate text is expressly prohibited. The author reserves all rights to license uses of this work for generative AI training and development of machine learning language models.

Michelle M. Pillow® is a registered trademark of The Raven Books LLC

ABOUT THE BOOK

LUNAR BOUND

Sci-fi Paranormal Romantic Comedy

He hunts in shadows. She shines a light he can't resist.

When three aliens crash into Duskrock, Arizona, empath and wildlife rehabilitator Poppy Jensen senses what no one else can—Lunar, a shadow-born operative from Zorveya's night side, made to move unseen. He expects fear. She offers a hand. One touch sparks more than either imagined, and suddenly secrecy is impossible.

Lunar never wanted to join Galaxy Alien Mail Order Brides on this ill-conceived mission, but his leaders gave him no choice. Now stranded on a strange planet and hunted by a ruthless black-ops outfit, survival depends on a woman who should never have been able to see him at all.

On the run through desert nights and hidden caves, forced proximity fans their connection into something undeniable. Lunar speaks in actions, and Poppy understands every one. With hunters closing in and extraction running out of time, he must decide if protecting his mission is worth losing the one woman who makes the darkness feel like home.

--

LUNAR BOUND is a steamy sci-fi paranormal romantic comedy with a grumpy alien and a sunshine empath, shadow-walking danger, hunted lovers on the run, sizzling open-door heat, and a guaranteed HEA with no cliffhanger.

Book three of the Bound Trilogy installment from the Galaxy Alien Mail Order Brides series.

GALAXY ALIEN MAIL ORDER BRIDES

HAVE YOU READ THEM ALL?

Spark

Flame

Blaze

Ice

Frost

Snow

Eclipse Bound

Solar Bound

Lunar Bound

WELCOME TO QURILIXEN

QURILIXEN WORLD NOVELS

Dragon Lords Series

Barbarian Prince

Perfect Prince

Dark Prince

Warrior Prince

His Highness The Duke

The Stubborn Lord

The Reluctant Lord

The Impatient Lord

The Dragon's Queen

Lords of the Var Series

The Savage King

The Playful Prince
The Bound Prince
The Rogue Prince
The Pirate Prince

Captured by a Dragon-Shifter Series

Determined Prince
Rebellious Prince
Stranded with the Cajun
Hunted by the Dragon
Mischievous Prince
Headstrong Prince

Space Lords Series

His Frost Maiden
His Fire Maiden
His Metal Maiden
His Earth Maiden
His Woodland Maiden

Dynasty Lords Series

Seduction of the Phoenix

Temptation of the Butterfly

To learn more about the Qurilixen World series of books and to stay up to date on the latest book list visit www.MichellePillow.com

AUTHOR UPDATES

To stay informed about when a new book in the series installments is released, sign up for updates:

michellepillow.com/author-updates

WELCOME TO GALAXY BRIDES

A NOTE FROM THE AUTHOR

Dear Readers,

For those of you familiar with my bestselling series, Dragon Lords, you've already been introduced to the Galaxy Brides Corporation and the services they offer lonely men and women of the future. What you might not have known is that Galaxy Brides (formerly aka "Galaxy Alien Mail Order Brides") dabbled in taking grooms to destinations—namely Earth! Unfortunately, they found the alien males a little too hard to control once they landed on our surface.

I hope you have as much fun reading this series as I've had writing it!

Happy Reading!

Michelle M. Pillow

To My Readers,
For always being willing to take that next adventure
with me.

PLANET OF ZORVEYA

Luniaren moved silently through the shadows of the transport bay, recording his thoughts in the privacy of his mind where they would remain untainted by the opinions of others. If this mission failed, which it would most assuredly do, he would not be blamed for it. He would not lose his ticket back home.

PERSONAL LOG, Pre-Departure:

This mission is a farce. A desperate ploy by a Peacemaker Council that has run out of rational options. I have been ordered to participate in this Galaxy Alien Mail Order Brides experiment, as if finding a mate on a primitive planet could somehow prove that generations of conflict between the light and shadow zones of Zorveya are merely a misunderstanding that can be resolved with goodwill.

Let me be clear. I have no intention of mating with fleshy aliens. I find the possibility disgusting.

My opposition has been noted and ignored. The punishments for refusal have been made clear: exile, the stripping of my family's land holdings in the shadow territories, and the dismantling of our ancestral research facilities. I go not by choice but by coercion.

My traveling companions are no better than expected. Solarestabinian, Solar Bound as they now insist on calling him, is the typical Solarus brute, all flash and fire with no subtlety. He is the sole representative of the light-dwellers of our tidal locked planet. And Eclipsyionic, Eclipse Bound, true to his twilight existence between dark and light, is forever balanced on the fence between our worlds, pretending neutrality while clearly favoring the light-dwellers with his policies. At least he has the decency to appear as uncomfortable with this arrangement as I am.

They call me Lunar Bound, which is an insulting designation. The Earth people use a surname to designate family. I will never be family to a light-dweller.

The Galaxy Alien Mail Order Brides corporation's representatives, Gary and Bob, are incompetent to a degree that borders on criminal negligence. Their ship appears to be cobbled together from spare parts, their knowledge of interspecies relations is superficial at best, and their understanding of our cultural conflicts is nonexistent. Someone should investigate how they were selected for such a significant undertaking.

I predict disaster. But I will observe. I will adapt. And I will survive, as those of the shadow have always done.

A FLASH of golden light interrupted his thoughts as Solar strutted into the transport bay, trailing energy sparks like a careless child. Lunar retreated deeper into the darkness, his night-adapted eyes narrowing against the unwelcome brightness.

"Ah, lurking in the shadows as usual," Solar called out, his voice deliberately loud. "Come into the light, Lunar. It's good for the complexion."

Lunar didn't dignify the taunt with a response. Solar knew perfectly well that extended exposure to his level of light output was harmful to shadow-dwellers. It was a petty provocation, designed to establish dominance before their journey even began.

What Solar didn't seem to realize was that deep space was dark. This ride would not be enjoyable for him. It might even be painful.

Lunar suppressed a smile at the thought.

Eclipse arrived next, his presence marking a balance between them as it always did. "Are you both prepared for departure?" he asked, placing his modest luggage beside the entry ramp.

"As prepared as one can be for a mission doomed to failure," Lunar replied quietly.

Solar scoffed. "For once, we agree. This is beneath my station as an Elite Guard. I should be overseeing the plasma cannon installations on the eastern border, not playing matchmaker on a backward planet."

"The council feels this diplomatic initiative has merit," Eclipse reminded them. "And our compliance is not optional."

"The council," Solar mimicked with a sneer, "hasn't set foot outside the Twilight Belt in generations. What do they know of the real tensions between our peoples?"

Lunar found himself in the uncomfortable position of sharing Solar's sentiment, if not his crude expression of it. The Peacemaker Council, with their compromise solutions and moderate stances, understood neither the depth of the shadow-dwellers' grievances nor the extent of the light-bearers' aggression.

"The ship is prepared for boarding," Bob announced, appearing suddenly at the top of the ramp. His yellow skin looked sickly even to Lunar's eyes, and the ill-fitting uniform he wore did nothing to inspire confidence.

The Galaxy Bride crew consisted of three short, strange alien creatures with oversized heads and eyes. Their energy signatures were all but nonexistent. Logic said that a head that size would hold vast knowledge. Lunar didn't think logic applied in this situation. Their hosts' heads seemed to be filled with empty space.

"We're just finishing the final checks on the navigation systems," Bob continued.

"By we, you mean the trainee who didn't have the sense to keep out of the night bogs, don't you?" Solar asked, his light pulsing with suspicion.

"Harris is fully qualified," Bob assured them unconvincingly. "Mostly. He's completed nearly sixty percent of his certification."

Lunar exchanged a glance with Eclipse, whose expression mirrored his own concern.

"I've updated my final arrangements," Solar announced with theatrical gravity. "In the event of my death during this mission, my belongings are to be distributed among my siblings, with the exception of my ceremonial blade, which should be used to stab Bob repeatedly."

"Always with the jokes," Bob laughed nervously. "Come aboard, come aboard! We have a schedule to maintain."

They boarded the ship in silence, each lost in their own thoughts. Lunar noted the shabby interior, the mismatched control panels, and the lingering smell of something burning. This vessel had seen better days, probably centuries ago.

"Your quarters are through here," Bob guided them to a small compartment with three narrow sleep platforms. "Cozy, isn't it?"

Solar immediately claimed the platform nearest the external wall, where a small porthole would allow him to absorb light during their journey. "I require this position," he declared, daring them to challenge him.

Lunar took the platform farthest from Solar's, in the darkest corner of the compartment. Eclipse, predictably, settled for the middle one with a resigned sigh.

"I will require something to block light," Lunar stated, glancing at his glowing bunkmate.

"Excellent!" Bob clapped his hands together. "Now, we've prepared information packets about Earth culture, mating rituals, and appropriate conversational topics. You will have plenty of time to absorb the information during the flight. Did you know humans consider discussion of bodily functions to be taboo in many social situations? Fascinating species."

"When do we see our potential mates?" Solar demanded. "I want to review my options."

"Oh, the matchmaking process happens on Earth," Bob explained. "Our new proprietary compatibility implants work best in proximity to the subjects. You'll be matched with females whose biorhythms complement your own unique energy signatures."

They did not need implants to tell them what they would know naturally. Matching energies was a science. Either they did or they didn't.

"And if no suitable matches are found?" Lunar asked, speaking the question that had been troubling him since this mission was announced.

Bob's smile faltered slightly. "Well, technically, the contract requires good-faith participation in the matching process for a minimum of one Earth month. After that, if no connections have been formed, we can discuss alternatives."

"Meaning we're stuck there for at least a month regardless," Solar concluded darkly.

"Think of it as a cultural exchange," Bob suggested brightly. "A chance to experience new customs, new foods, new social structures."

"I think of it as exile," Lunar said softly, though only Eclipse seemed to hear him.

The ship's engines rumbled to life, vibrating through the floor in a way that did not inspire confidence in their structural integrity. A voice that must belong to the trainee Harris crackled over the communication system.

"Preparing for departure. Please secure all personal items and fasten safety restraints."

Solar muttered something uncomplimentary about Harris' parentage as they made their way to the main cabin for takeoff. The chairs were mismatched, as if salvaged from different vessels, but they all appeared to have functional restraints.

As Lunar secured himself in the chair farthest from the viewports, he caught sight of the Peace-maker Council representatives watching from the observation deck. Their grim expressions were solemn. Not the look of officials sending diplomats on a hopeful mission, but of jailers dispatching prisoners to a remote colony.

Lunar realized the council didn't expect them to succeed. They were removing them from the equation to prevent them from influencing the upcoming conflict.

The implications were troubling. If the council believed war was inevitable, this mission wasn't a peace initiative. It was a convenient way to eliminate three influential figures from opposing factions before hostilities began.

The engines roared louder, drowning out Bob's cheerful commentary about the wonders of interstellar travel. The ship shuddered as it lifted from the platform, lurching sideways in a manner that suggested Harris' nearly sixty percent of certification was being generously rounded up.

"Is this normal?" Solar demanded as the vessel banked sharply, sending loose items sliding across the floor.

"Absolutely!" Bob assured them, though his knuckles had turned a paler shade of yellow as he gripped his own restraints. "Just a bit of turbulence. Very common during orbital departure."

Lunar closed his eyes, focusing on the techniques his people used to remain calm in crisis. The shadow-dwellers had survived centuries of hardship by adapting, by finding advantages in situations others considered hopeless. He would do the same.

When he opened his eyes again, they had cleared the atmosphere, and the blackness of space surrounded them. Here, at least, he felt more comfortable. The darkness between stars was familiar territory.

"Now then," Gary appeared from the pilot's cabin, looking harried. "Let's discuss the finer points of your Earth experience. We've selected a location called Duskrock, Arizona, which is known for its spiritual energy and openness to unusual visitors."

"Meaning they won't immediately report us to authorities when we display non-human traits," Eclipse translated.

"Exactly," Gary confirmed with disturbing cheer. "The locals have a long history of believing in extraterrestrial visitation. Many of them actively seek it out. You'll blend right in. We believe this will greatly increase your chances of mating. Unlike some of the more troubling locations we tried in the past."

"With this?" Solar gestured to his golden, light-emitting skin. "How exactly?"

"We've prepared skin-suits for public use," Gary explained, producing what appeared to be thin, flesh-colored membranes from a storage compartment. "The latest models. Almost completely convincing unless examined very closely."

Lunar accepted the skin-suit with distaste. It felt unpleasantly organic between his fingers, designed to mask his natural shadow-absorption capabilities with a dull, human-like exterior. The thought of wearing it made his skin crawl, but he understood the necessity.

"And our accommodations?" Eclipse inquired.

"We will secure lodging at a local establishment," Gary said. "I hear the room is very nice."

"One room?" Solar's skin flared so brightly that Lunar had to shield his eyes. "For all three of us? That will not do."

"Budget constraints," Gary explained with an apologetic shrug. "The corporation's profit margins have been tight since the Killian incident, and your council did not authorize the added expense of multiple dwellings."

Lunar's spirits, already low, sank further. Sharing quarters with Solar meant enduring constant light exposure, which would drain his energy and impair his abilities. But arguing was pointless. The decision had clearly been made without consideration for their biological needs.

He retreated into his thoughts, focusing on the

one aspect of this mission that held any interest, which was the opportunity to observe an unfamiliar species in their natural habitat. Lunar had always been a student of behavior patterns, finding that understanding others' motivations gave him an advantage in negotiations and conflicts. Perhaps he could use this forced exile to expand his knowledge.

The journey to Earth would take several cycles, during which they were expected to study the information packets and practice their human mannerisms. Lunar intended to use the time more productively, analyzing the ship's systems for weaknesses and mapping escape routes through the stars in case the need arose.

As Solar and Eclipse engaged in yet another pointless argument about sleeping arrangements, Lunar slipped away to the small viewing port at the rear of the vessel. Zorveya was already a distant point of light, its distinctive half-bright, half-dark appearance lost among the stars.

He placed his hand against the cold surface of the port, a rare moment of sentiment for one of his kind.

PERSONAL LOG, *Departure:*

We are now committed to this path. I have left instructions with my family regarding the protection of our territories in the event of hostilities escalating during my absence. They will do what is necessary.

I do not expect to find a bride on Earth. The concept is absurd. I have read what they have given us about the women. What human female would willingly bind herself to a being from the shadows, one whose natural state would terrify her delicate senses? But I will participate in this charade as required, if only to ensure my eventual return.

My true mission, self-assigned, is to gather information. Earth may be primitive, but all species have strengths that can be leveraged. Perhaps they possess resources or technologies that could benefit the shadow territories in the coming conflict.

And if, as I suspect, this mission is merely a convenient exile to remove us from Zorveya during critical negotiations, then I will use the time to prepare for what comes after. The council has underestimated me if they believe distance will reduce my influence.

The shadows reach everywhere, even across the stars.

. . .

HE TURNED AWAY from the viewport, composing his features into the neutral mask he typically wore. As he moved back through the ship, staying close to the walls where the lighting was dimmest, he noticed something peculiar.

A small, metallic object had fallen from Gary's pocket during the turbulent departure. It was a data storage device of some kind, its design unfamiliar. Lunar retrieved it silently, slipping it into his own pocket without breaking stride.

Information was power, and he intended to acquire as much of it as possible before this mission reached its inevitable, disappointing conclusion.

When he returned to the main cabin, Solar was demonstrating his combat techniques to an uncomfortable-looking Bob, while Eclipse mediated yet another misunderstanding about luggage allowances. None of them noticed Lunar's brief absence, which was exactly as he preferred it.

The shadow-dweller settled into his seat, watching and listening as he always did. Patience was the virtue his people valued above all others. He would wait, observe, and adapt.

Earth might be a primitive planet, but every world had secrets worth discovering. And Lunar was very, very good at discovering secrets.

2

CRIMSON ROCK INN, DUSKROCK, ARIZONA, *Planet Earth, One Earth Month Later...*

Pure darkness did not exist in this human dwelling.

Lunar stood in the corner of the hotel room where the shadows were densest, but even here, light leaked in persistently. It came in the form of sunlight from the window that Solar refused to cover, in the artificial illumination from the blinking devices, and even the glow from Solar's skin as he basked near the window like a hatchling in its first light cycle.

What did he do to deserve this Earth hell?

The room was basic and crude. Two sleeping platforms, draped in synthetic fabrics, occupied the space. The walls, made of thin material, offered no defense against attacks. A humming cooling unit, used for food preservation, emitted a frequency that could drive shadow-dwellers into madness. Most unsettling of all, there were no private areas where true darkness could be found.

PERSONAL LOG, *Earth Arrival:*

We have survived the incompetence of Galaxy Alien Mail Order Brides and their trainee pilot. Our landing was catastrophic by any reasonable standard. The craft is damaged beyond repair by my assessment. Our supplies are all but lost. Our communication with the corporation representatives is intermittent at best. I suspect this was by design rather than accidental.

Earth is brighter than I hoped. Even their night cycle offers minimal relief with artificial illumination scattered throughout their settlements. My energy reserves are already being depleted from constant exposure to light. I estimate I can maintain full functionality for approximately seven Earth days before requiring deep shadow immersion.

Eclipse has secured temporary accommodations at a structure known as the Crimson Rock Inn. The name is misleading as it is not crimson, nor is the building made of rock. Solar has claimed the area nearest the window, maximizing my discomfort. Eclipse mediates as usual, accomplishing nothing.

"Are you planning to lurk in that corner all day, night-crawler? Even humans will find that suspicious." Solar's voice intruded on his thoughts.

"I am observing," Lunar replied, not bothering to emerge from his position. "Our mission requires understanding Earth customs before interaction. Perhaps you should try it instead of glowing like a distress beacon desperate for attention."

Solar scoffed, his skin brightening in irritation. The electronic devices in the room flickered in response. "I'm absorbing energy. Unlike you, I require light to function properly."

"Both of you, lower your voices," Eclipse cautioned from his position by the door. He had been examining the primitive locking mechanism with undisguised concern. "These walls are not secured. Anyone could be listening."

Lunar had already determined the room's vulnerabilities within minutes of arrival. The door lock could be bypassed with minimal effort. The window latch was equally inadequate, not that it would take much to breach the glass. The ventilation system provided multiple access points for surveillance devices. Humans apparently lived in constant exposure to both elements and to one another.

"I require darkness," Lunar stated flatly.

"Not happening," Solar replied. "Unless, Eclipse, we can inject him into deep space?"

Eclipse sighed, the sound familiar after cycles of the same argument. "We need to adapt to local conditions. According to the information packet, humans typically sleep during their night cycle and are active during daylight. We should attempt to follow this pattern to blend in."

That sounded like a horrible idea.

"Adaptation?" Lunar moved deeper into his corner as Solar deliberately flared brighter. "How am I to adapt when sharing quarters with a living light source? You cannot expect me to walk around in constant light."

Instead of answering, Eclipse picked up a small rectangular device left in the bag by the handlers. He activated it, revealing a primitive data display. "This will give us directions and provide access to electronic currency. We should acquire necessities before establishing contact with potential mates."

"I'm not sharing a sleeping platform with the

shadow," Solar declared, gesturing to the two beds. "He'll probably try to smother me in my sleep."

"If I wanted to eliminate you," Lunar countered, "I wouldn't wait until you were sleeping."

Eclipse moved between them, holding up his hands. "No one is eliminating anyone. We will construct a sleeping arrangement for Lunar in the bathing chamber where it's darker."

He found the compromise acceptable. The bathing chamber was the only partially tolerable space in the dwelling, a small room with no windows where Lunar might find relief from constant illumination. Well, except for the blinking red light on the ceiling device. Regardless, sharing such confined quarters with Solar would be insufferable.

"I will conduct reconnaissance," Lunar announced, pushing away from his corner. "This settlement must have areas of adequate darkness."

"You can't go wandering off alone," Eclipse protested. "We need to maintain a unified presence."

"I will not be detected," Lunar assured him, already moving toward the door. His shadow-walking abilities were unmatched even among his own kind. On this primitive world with its inadequate security systems, he would be virtually invisible.

Solar snorted. "Let him go. Maybe he'll find a cave to hide in. More room for us."

"Lunar," Eclipse's voice took on its diplomatic tone, the one that normally preceded unwelcome compromises. "At least wear the skin-suit if you leave. Your natural appearance will draw attention."

The skin-suit was repulsive. The thin membrane was designed to mask his shadow-absorbing skin with a dull human-like exterior. Wearing it felt like being wrapped in a layer of congealed oil.

With reluctance, Lunar retrieved the skin-suit from the travel bag. He retreated to the bathing chamber to apply it, wanting privacy for the undignified process. The mirror reflected his true form, tall and lean, with skin that absorbed light rather than reflected it, creating a perpetual shadow effect around his body.

The skin-suit covered this distinctive feature, transforming him into a dull, ordinary-looking human. His shadow-walking abilities would be diminished while wearing it, but not eliminated entirely. Still, it was a necessary compromise. He pulled the baggy one-piece over the skin.

When he emerged, Solar laughed. "You look terrible. Like a corpse animated by Franktonian scientists."

Eclipse interrupted, holding up more Earthman garments that had been provided. "These coverings are insufficient. We'll need to acquire something to blend in properly." He presented a piece of paper with crude markings. "There appears to be a commercial district within walking distance."

"I'll join you later," Lunar stated, moving toward the door. "After I check the perimeter."

"Don't get lost in the shadows," Solar called after him. "I'd hate to have to come rescue you from Earth's law enforcement."

Lunar didn't bother responding. Solar's provocations were as predictable as they were tiresome.

The corridor outside their room was mercifully dimmer than their quarters, though still brighter than any shadow-dweller would find comfortable. Lunar moved quickly, keeping to the walls where the lighting was less intense. The building's layout was simple. It consisted of a central hallway with rooms branching off on either side, and a stairwell at each end.

He avoided the main exit, instead locating a service door that led to an exterior area behind the building. This space was cluttered with waste receptacles and maintenance equipment, but more importantly, it was partially shaded by the structure itself.

Earth's sun hung low in the sky, marking late afternoon by human standards. The dry, warm air carried unfamiliar smells. Lunar took a deep breath. He isolated the mineral makeup of the soil, the native plants, and the faint chemical traces from human habitats.

Movement caught his attention. A small creature scurried across the ground, pausing to examine him with wary eyes before disappearing into the underbrush. It was some form of local wildlife that had adapted to living in proximity to humans.

Interesting. Perhaps not all Earth species lacked survival instincts.

Lunar moved deeper into the shade, allowing himself to merge with the shadows. Despite the skinsuit limiting his abilities, he managed to disappear from human perception when there was darkness to draw from. He started to walk around the building, keeping near the walls and watching quietly without drawing attention.

Humans went about their activities unaware of being observed. They entered and exited vehicles powered by combustion, not gravity manipulation. They carried packages and communicated via handheld devices, which seemed to be issued to most. Many wore protective eye coverings to shield their eyes from the sun's radiation. Although this seemed like an evolutionary flaw, Lunar silently slipped past a group and took a pair of glasses from someone's head without being noticed. The dark lenses helped.

He continued his reconnaissance, circling the entire Crimson Rock structure before expanding outward to survey the surrounding area. The settlement was built among unusual rock formations of striking red coloration. Natural energy convergences might explain the humans' choice of location, though their technologies appeared too primitive to detect or utilize such resources.

One human female caught his attention specifically. She moved with purpose between buildings, carrying an injured animal in her arms. Unlike the others, she didn't speak into devices or move with the distracted gait of those absorbed in their own concerns. Her focus was entirely on the creature she held, as she murmured soothingly to it.

The animal, some small, furry quadruped, appeared to be in distress. Yet instead of eliminating the weakened creature, the female was clearly providing care. An interesting behavior pattern. Inefficient from an evolutionary perspective, but perhaps indicative of social structures worth studying.

Lunar followed at a distance, his curiosity

piqued. The female entered a building labeled "Desert Animal Rescue" and disappeared inside. Through the window, he could see her carefully placing the animal on a treatment surface while another human approached with what appeared to be medical implements.

Caring for non-sentient species, he noted mentally. *This empathy response could be exploited.*

Her eyes lifted, and she stared out the window in his direction like she could see him. That was impossible, of course. A current ran through his body. Lunar retreated into the shadows.

He left the mysterious woman to continue exploring the settlement. As darkness finally fell, Lunar felt his strength returning. Earth's night offered him a chance to move more freely without the skin-suit. He located several promising areas of deep shadow and chose a narrow space between buildings to strip out of the disguise. He hid the outfit so he could retrieve it later before meeting back up with Eclipse and Solar. He didn't need them knowing that he wandered the planet uncovered.

When he emerged from the alley, it was in a dark area by a social gathering place named The Crash Zone. This location proved most interesting. Humans were entering the front of the building in significant numbers, many wearing garments deco-rated with crude representations of extraterrestrial beings. Some even wore wrinkled metallic coverings on their heads, a puzzling choice with no obvious practical purpose.

Through a partially open door, Lunar glimpsed the interior. He swept through the shadows of the club undetected, only to exit on the other side. The space was dimly lit with strange-colored artificial lights, filled with people using substances and engaging in behaviors that seemed related to mating. So this was how Earth species initiated reproductive connections. Chaotic and inefficient, but potentially useful knowledge for their mission. It would be so much easier to tap into their personal biorhythms.

He was about to move on when a female emerged from the rear exit, separated from his posi-tion by only a narrow alley. He recognized her from earlier when she cared for the injured animal. She stepped into the dim light, breathing deeply as if the interior atmosphere had been unpleasant to her respiratory system.

Lunar froze, allowing his natural abilities to render him virtually invisible against the darkened wall. The woman should have continued on, unaware of his presence.

Instead, she turned directly toward him.

"Don't run away. I know you're there," she said, her voice carrying clearly through the still air. "I followed you from the clinic. I felt you watching me."

Impossible. No human should be able to detect a shadow-walker in darkness. Their visual systems were inadequate, their perception limited to basic electromagnetic wavelengths.

Yet this female looked directly at his position. Her eyes, unusual in coloration, almost luminous, seemed to pierce his concealment.

"It's okay," she said, stepping toward him instead of back, completely defying any survival instincts. "I'm not afraid. You don't have to hide."

Lunar remained perfectly still. Any movement would confirm his presence. The female was likely experiencing a perceptual anomaly, not actually detecting him.

She took another step forward, and Lunar noticed something unusual. The ambient light didn't reflect from her skin in the expected pattern. Instead, it seemed to be absorbed and redistributed, creating a subtle aura effect that his shadow-adapted vision could detect but ordinary human perception would miss.

"I'm Poppy," she said, still addressing the apparently empty darkness where he stood. "You're one of them, aren't you? One of the visitors who arrived today."

The corporation's information had mentioned nothing about humans with enhanced perception. This was an unexpected variable. Potentially dangerous. Definitely worthy of further study.

Before Lunar could decide on a course of action, the female reached into her garment and extracted a small object. She placed it carefully on the ground between them.

"A peace offering," she explained, stepping back. "It's a shadow stone. Black tourmaline. For protection and grounding. You seem like you could use both."

Then, most surprisingly of all, she smiled directly at him before turning and walking away, leaving the small dark object on the ground where she'd placed it.

Lunar remained motionless until she had disappeared around the corner of the building. Only then did he emerge from the shadows to examine what she'd left.

The object was indeed a stone, black and crystalline, cool to the touch. It was unremarkable by interplanetary standards, definitely not the sophisticated technology he had briefly suspected. Just a piece of mineral composite with no obvious purpose.

Yet she had given it specifically to him, an entity she shouldn't have been able to perceive.

PERSONAL LOG, *Supplemental:*

I have encountered a human female with unusual perceptual abilities. She detected my presence despite shadow concealment. This suggests some Earth humans may possess capabilities not documented in our briefing materials.

The female, self-identified as Poppy, displayed no fear response upon apparent detection of a non-Earth entity. Instead, she initiated a potential social exchange protocol, offering a mineral object of unknown significance.

This requires further investigation. If some humans can detect shadow-walkers, our mission parameters may need adjustment. Additionally, the female's unusual energy signature warrants closer observation. I will consider making contact with her under a more controlled setting.

I will return to the dwelling to evaluate this development. The mineral object will be analyzed for properties.

. . .

LUNAR KEPT the stone and made his way to his skin-suit and clothes before heading back to the Crimson Rock Inn, staying within the deep shadows of evening. This mission had just become marginally more interesting than expected.

Perhaps Earth wasn't entirely without secrets worth discovering after all.

3

Poppy Jensen had been feeling the changes since before dawn.

Something had shifted in Duskrock's usually stable energy field. Most people wouldn't realize it. Tourists visited for the vortexes without truly understanding them, and locals had become accustomed to the steady flow of spiritual vacationers and their crystal collections. But Poppy wasn't like most people.

She'd woken at 4:17 AM, the numbers on her bedside clock glowing as something pulled her from sleep. A disturbance. Not like an earthquake exactly, more like when someone dropped a stone into still water and the ripples spread outward, changing everything they touched.

Something was coming.

By mid-morning, her phone had exploded with texts about a UFO crash near Pete's crystal shop. Normally, she'd dismiss it as another Duskrock spectacle. This town had a UFO sighting every other weekend. But combined with what she'd felt, she couldn't ignore it. Something was calling to her, and she had to go to it.

"Moonbeam, can you cover for me this afternoon?" she asked her coworker at Desert Animal Rescue. Poppy worked there four days a week, rehabilitating injured wildlife. "I need to check something out."

Moonbeam, born Jessica but reborn as Moonbeam during a particularly intense peyote ceremony five years ago, nodded without looking up from the injured jackrabbit she was tending. "The crash vibes calling you, too?"

"Something like that," Poppy admitted.

By the time she arrived at Pete's, the fire was out and the crowd had dispersed, but the energy lingered. Standing near the doorway of Pete's shop, looking in at the scattered crystals, Poppy closed her eyes and let her other senses take over.

Cold. Dark. Watching.

The impression came so strongly that it made her

gasp. Someone observed from the shadows. Not malevolent, but different. Like nothing she'd ever felt before.

"Pretty wild, right?" Pete appeared beside her, grinning through his singed beard. "Told ya they'd come eventually."

"What exactly did you see?" Poppy asked, keeping her voice neutral. Pete was a true believer with a tendency to embellish.

"Ship came down right on my roof," he said, pointing up at the blackened rafters. "Three of 'em came down after the crash, right before it went up in flames. Well, four if you count the little one."

"Four beings?" she clarified, her skin tingling.

"Yep. One was bright, like he was made of sunlight. One was dark, kept to the shadows. And one in between, kinda purple-ish. Little guy looked human-ish but weird with a giant head. They took off that way." He pointed toward town.

Poppy nodded.

"Your shadow stones survived," Pete added, handing her a small cloth bag. "Thought you might want them, considering."

"Thanks, Pete." She slipped the bag into her pocket. Black tourmaline, her specialty. She resold them at the local market and kept a collection for herself. They were especially good for protection and grounding negative energies.

Throughout the afternoon, Poppy followed the energy signatures through town. The bright presence was easy to track. It left a trail of electrical disturbances and flickering lights. The shadow was harder, appearing and disappearing like a ghost, but she could sense it when she quieted her mind. Once she'd almost gotten close to finding the source of the dark energy, but an injured cat took her on a side quest to the clinic.

By evening, she found herself drawn to The Crash Zone, Duskrock's tackiest alien-themed bar. The irony wasn't lost on her that real extraterrestrials might actually visit a place decorated with inflatable aliens and UFO string lights.

Inside, the usual Friday crowd was amplified by tourists and locals eager to discuss the day's excitement. Stephanie from the yoga retreat was holding court, showing everyone her viral video of "I definitely caught aliens" while collecting free drinks from wide-eyed believers.

Poppy ordered a seltzer water and found a quiet corner to observe. The bar's dim lighting and neon accents created plenty of shadows, and she let her awareness expand outward, feeling for that distinctive cold presence. A shiver worked over her as a chill slipped past the overheated interior of the bar.

There.

Her senses followed it outside to the alley behind the bar. Waiting.

Setting her untouched drink aside, Poppy slipped through the crowd toward the rear exit. The night air felt cool on her skin after the stuffy bar interior. She took a deep breath, centering herself.

The presence was stronger now. Hiding in the deepest shadow against the wall, where the security light didn't reach. Most people would walk right past, seeing nothing. But Poppy had never been limited to physical sight.

"Don't run away. I know you're there," she said, keeping her voice gentle. "I followed you from the clinic. I felt you watching me."

No response, but the energy shifted slightly. Surprise, perhaps?

"It's okay," she continued, taking a step toward the darkness. Fear wasn't even an option in her mind. Whoever was hiding there wasn't a threat to her. "I'm not afraid. You don't have to hide."

The shadow remained perfectly still, but she could sense its focus intensifying. Studying her. Trying to understand how she'd detected it.

"I'm Poppy," she offered, trying to establish a connection. "You're one of them, aren't you? One of the visitors who arrived today."

She'd been sensitive to energies since childhood. Her grandmother had been the same way, talking to ghosts and holding seances. It was a mixed blessing in a town like Duskrock, where the veil between worlds felt thinner and energy signatures from tourists overwhelmed her until she learned to filter them out. But this was different. This energy was truly alien in a way that resonated with something deep inside her.

The shadow neither confirmed nor denied her words. But she knew. Of course, she knew.

Reaching into her pocket, Poppy pulled out one of the black tourmaline stones Pete had saved for her. It was perfect for someone who lived in darkness, who might need grounding in this chaotic world of humans.

"A peace offering," she explained, placing it carefully on the ground between them before stepping back. "It's a shadow stone. Black tourmaline. For protection and grounding. You seem like you could use both."

She smiled directly at the presence she couldn't quite see but absolutely felt, then turned and walked away. The encounter felt incomplete, but pushing further might scare it away. Better to establish trust slowly.

As she rounded the corner of the building, her heart raced with excitement and validation. After a lifetime of sensing things others couldn't, of being called too sensitive or over imaginative, she'd finally found proof that her perceptions were real.

They were here. They were real. And at least one of them resonated with shadows in a way that called to her own affinity for the spaces between light.

Poppy didn't go back into the bar. Instead, she walked the quiet streets, letting the night air cool her flushed face. Her mind kept returning to that shadow presence. The stillness of it, the watching, the complete absence of light. Not evil, not at all. Just different. Like a piece of night sky had detached itself and taken form.

Her phone buzzed with a text from her room-mate, *"Crash Zone packed with alien nuts. Heading home.*

"On my way," she replied. *"Got another rescue coming in tomorrow. Early start."*

The rescue center was expecting a coyote pup that had been found abandoned near one of the hiking trails. Another creature needing gentle handling and safe shadows to recover in. Poppy specialized in nocturnal animals, those that shied away from human contact and preferred darkness. Her coworkers joked that she spoke night creature fluently.

Maybe that's why she'd been able to sense the shadow visitor. Like recognized like.

Her small cottage sat on the outskirts of town, where light pollution was minimal and the stars shone brighter. She shared it with Kai, another rescue worker, though their schedules rarely overlapped. The arrangement provided her with the solitude she needed after days spent dealing with others.

Tonight, the cottage was dark except for the small lamp Kai always left on for her. Poppy moved through the rooms without turning on additional lights, comfortable in the dimness. Her bedroom was her sanctuary. The walls were painted deep indigo. She had blackout curtains and a collection of stones arranged on shelves and windowsills.

She changed into loose cotton pants and a tank top, then sat cross-legged on her bed, closing her eyes to center herself. The day's events had left her buzzing with excess energy that needed grounding.

As she breathed deeply, focusing on the sensation of roots growing from her body into the earth below, Poppy felt it again. The distinct cold presence observed her from a distance. Not inside her home, but somewhere outside, watching.

Instead of fear, she felt a surprising sense of recognition. Of connection.

Opening her eyes, Poppy moved to her window and pulled back the curtain just enough to peer outside. The yard was dark, the trees creating deeper patches of shadow against the night sky.

"I know you're still there," she whispered, though she doubted he could hear her through the glass. "It's okay. I understand needing the darkness."

She placed her palm flat against the window, a gesture of acceptance. Then she closed the curtain again, respecting the watcher's desire for privacy.

Tomorrow, she would bring an offering to the Crimson Rock Inn, where Mike's friend had reported seeing strange new guests checking in. A proper welcome basket filled with some local foods, a map of the area's shadiest spots, and more black tourmaline. It would be a peace offering from one shadow-friend to another.

Poppy slipped into her bed, dimming her bedside lamp to its lowest setting before turning it off completely. In the perfect darkness, she smiled.

For years she'd felt out of place among Duskrock's sun-worshippers. Her sensitivity to energy made her good at her work, but often left her drained and seeking solitude. Even in this community of spiritualists and seekers, she'd always been just a little too strange, a little too attuned to things others couldn't perceive.

But now, something from beyond the stars had arrived. Something that understood shadows. And it had noticed her too.

In the morning, she would begin her search in earnest. But for now, she rested, content in the knowledge that she was no longer alone in her affinity for darkness.

Sleep came easily, and her dreams were filled with stars that absorbed light rather than emitted it, and eyes that watched from the spaces between worlds.

4

LUNAR HAD NOT PLANNED TO BE DISCOVERED.

The fact that she saw him was a blow to his ego.

He couldn't stop thinking about it.

No, her. He couldn't stop thinking about *her*.

Shadow-walking was an art form on Zorveya, perfected through generations of necessity. Light-dwellers dominated the planet's resources, forcing those of the shadow to develop stealth techniques for survival. Lunar was considered exceptionally skilled, even among his own kind. Yet somehow, this Earth female had perceived him where countless others had failed.

After his encounter with Poppy, Lunar had spent hours analyzing the small black stone she'd given him. The object possessed unusual properties, absorbing ambient energy in a pattern similar to his own shadow manipulation. Not advanced technology, merely a natural mineral with convenient attributes. Yet she had selected it specifically for him.

Fascinating.

Morning had found him restless in the inadequate Crimson Rock accommodations. He hid from the others. Solar's constant emissions made proper rest impossible, and Eclipse's diplomatic hovering only added to his irritation. When Solar finally left to check the continental breakfast, Lunar had slipped out without announcement. His actions needed no explanation or permission.

He tracked Poppy's energy signature to a building identified as Desert Animal Rescue, where she appeared to be caring for injured non-sentient creatures. He'd been drawn to this place before and found it to be an unusual occupation, but one that suggested useful skills for survival. Patience. Caution. Understanding of biological needs.

After observing her routine for approximately two Earth hours, Lunar had followed her to another location, the Duskrock Yoga and Spa Meditation Center. The facility's design offered abundant shadows for concealment, allowing him to move undetected through its corridors while observing human behaviors.

Or so he had believed.

"I can feel you," Poppy's voice called softly as she stepped into an empty room. The compact space was stocked with supplies and unusual Earth food holding artifacts. "You don't have to hide from me."

Lunar remained in shadow, calculating options. Retreat was logical. Engagement threatened the mission's success. Curiosity, an instinct his shadowy ancestors had fostered as vital for survival, urged him to stay.

"I know you've been following me today. Show yourself," Poppy said louder.

Lunar kept watching, observing her closely. Her form was pleasing, so delicate. And her emotions calmly washed over him. She wasn't chaotic like the other humans.

"Do you understand me?" Her eyes searched the shadows. "Please, say something."

"How do you perceive me?" he asked finally, maintaining his shadow form rather than stepping into visibility.

Poppy appeared relieved to hear his voice emerging from the darkness. "I sense energy patterns.

Yours is distinct. Like a void that moves with purpose."

"Most humans lack this capacity," Lunar observed.

"Most, yes." She smiled slightly. "I take after my grandmother. We've always been sensitive to what she would call shadow frequencies."

"Shadow frequencies," Lunar repeated. The terminology was primitive but conceptually accurate. "Your species classification system does not include such perceptual ranges."

"I'm an anomaly." She took a step closer to his position, her eyes not quite focusing on where he actually stood, but impressively close. "The stone I gave you last night, did it help?"

"It's not safe for you to know about me," Lunar replied. Solar and Eclipse would not be happy about this.

"I can't help who I am," Poppy said. "You can trust me."

Before Lunar could respond, the door burst open, flooding the space with light that disrupted his shadow form. Solar stood in the doorway, his irritated glow barely contained by the deteriorating skin-suit. Golden energy spilled from the edges.

"You," Poppy whispered, looking at Solar. "You're the bright one. From the crash."

Solar ignored her, focusing on Lunar. "Eclipse sent me. We must go to our assigned dwelling. You should not be talking to anyone."

"This human has unusual perceptive abilities," Lunar replied coldly, refusing to be treated like an errant child. "She detected my presence despite shadow concealment."

"That doesn't matter," Solar insisted, his skin brightening with typical arrogance. The room's lighting fixtures began to flicker and buzz with his uncontrolled emissions. "Eclipse has secured new accommodations."

Poppy seemed unaffected by Solar's display, her attention returning to Lunar. "The shadow stones should help. I have more if you need them."

Solar's attention snapped to her. "What do you know of us?"

Poppy met his gaze without fear. "I know you're not from here. I know you crashed near Pete's shop yesterday. I know you're different from each other, light and shadow." She gestured toward them. "And I know you can manipulate energy to the point you're disrupting the retreat's electrical system."

The overhead light exploded in a shower of

sparks as if to confirm her assessment. She gave a small yelp of surprise and jumped out of the way of falling glass.

"Poppy has offered assistance," Lunar explained to Solar, willing the Solarian for once in his life to be calm.

"Poppy?" Solar repeated, his tone suggesting disbelief. "You revealed yourself to a human without authorization. Have you forgotten our mission parameters?"

"I revealed nothing," Lunar countered, finding Solar's hypocrisy typical. "She perceived me through means I have yet to determine."

Poppy stepped forward, her posture suggesting a mediating intent similar to Eclipse's habitual interventions. "Look, I don't want to cause trouble. I just want to help. Duskrock can be overwhelming for sensitive beings."

Lunar hid his amusement at the fact that she called Solar sensitive. It wasn't a compliment.

"We do not require your assistance," Solar stated with characteristic dismissal. "And I am not sensitive."

Poppy gave him a bemused look. "Really? Because from where I'm standing, you two can barely be in the same room without causing electrical failures. That seems like something that might draw attention."

The lights began to flicker. Lunar automatically reacted to Solar's wave of heat. He lowered the temperature in the room, summoning the shadows. If the hot-headed Solar wanted a fight, he'd give him one. After being trapped with him for months on a spaceship, Lunar had met his limit.

Eclipse burst into the room with a human female, the coordinator from the crash site. "Both of you, control yourselves. You're causing an outage."

"I tracked the shadow-dweller as instructed," Solar replied with unnecessary self-importance. "He was engaged in unauthorized contact with this human."

"I was conducting necessary reconnaissance," Lunar corrected, refusing to be characterized as disobedient when his actions had a strategic purpose.

Eclipse turned his attention to Poppy.

"Hi. I'm Poppy Jensen. I work at Desert Animal Rescue," she answered with remarkable composure. "I felt your arrival yesterday. I gave your friend here a shadow stone last night when I sensed him outside The Crash Zone."

Solar glared at him. "You attended the human

gathering place without informing us and made contact?"

"I was not aware I needed permission to conduct independent exploration," Lunar replied, deliberately allowing his shadows to deepen. The room's temperature dropped several more degrees. Solar's response was predictable. The remaining functional lights pulsed erratically.

"I have a suite reserved for you," Solar's friend interjected. "Private entrance, separate bedrooms, minimal staff interaction. But we need to get you there now before someone calls the electrical company about the power surges."

"You trust this human?" Lunar asked Eclipse.

"You can call me Rowan," she said.

"Yes," Eclipse said without hesitation. Lunar noted the emotional indicators in Eclipse's tone. The twilight-dweller had formed an attachment to this human female after less than one planetary rotation. Fascinating, if potentially problematic for mission objectives.

"Fine," Solar interrupted, always needing to act like he had authority. "Lead us to this suite."

"I wish to speak further with Poppy," Lunar stated.

"You can do so later," Eclipse ordered. "After we've relocated to a more secure area."

Lunar observed Poppy retrieving another black stone from her pocket, identical to the one she had given him. She offered it to Solar.

"Black tourmaline," she explained. "It absorbs negative energy. You might find it helpful for dampening your output."

Solar hesitated. Lunar stiffened, ready to defend Poppy if Solar insulted her. Finally, Solar accepted the stone.

He detected the subtle energy shift as the mineral began absorbing Solar's excess emissions. The effectiveness of these natural Earth minerals was unexpected and potentially valuable information.

He wondered how many stones Poppy could get her hands on. He'd like to bury Solar under a pile of them.

"We need to go now," Rowan insisted, checking her communication device. "Stephanie just texted me. The maintenance crew is heading this way to check the electrical panel."

Eclipse nodded. "Solar, Lunar, follow us. And please, try to maintain your human appearance."

As they exited the room, Lunar positioned

himself close to the walls where shadows were deepest. He observed Poppy naturally walking next to him, keeping distance while staying within communication range. She adjusted her pace to match his, showing careful attention to his movement patterns.

"The desert has deep shadows at night," she said quietly as they followed the others through a service corridor. "Caves where sunlight never reaches. Places where you might properly rest."

Lunar glanced at her. "You suggest locations for recuperation without knowing my physiological requirements."

"I work with nocturnal animals," Poppy replied. "Creatures that thrive in darkness. The shadows speak to them differently than light." She paused. "They speak to me too."

Before Lunar could respond, they emerged outside into bright sunlight. He instinctively withdrew deeper into his skin-suit, the discomfort immediate and intense. Poppy noticed his reaction and subtly positioned herself to cast additional shadow along their path.

"The suite was originally designed for celebrity guests who wanted privacy," Rowan explained as they walked.

Lunar focused on making his way toward the shade, ignoring the others as they continued talking.

They approached a structure partially embedded in the red rock formations. Lunar assessed its defensive capabilities. There were few entry points, natural concealment, and a strategic height advantage. It was more secure than Crimson Rock Inn across all measures.

Rowan unlocked the door, revealing interior spaces with distinct light and shadow zones. Lunar immediately identified the optimal position. The western sleeping room had minimal light exposure.

"The east-facing room gets morning sun," Rowan explained, gesturing to Solar. "The west room stays shaded most of the day and has blackout curtains," she added, indicating the area Lunar had already selected. "And the center room has adjustable lighting."

The accommodations suggested a specific design for their physiological needs. Either a remarkable coincidence or evidence of the human's perceptive abilities. Neither option aligned with their briefing materials on Earth's technological development.

"I'll leave you to get settled," Rowan said, placing control keys on a surface. "There's a private entrance code for the gate. No one will disturb you here."

"I should go as well," Poppy said, glancing at Lunar. "But I'd like to bring you something tomorrow. A proper welcome basket."

"That would be acceptable," Lunar replied before Eclipse or Solar could object. Additional interaction with this human would provide valuable data.

Once they were alone, tension rolled between them. Lunar felt an argument brewing.

"Convenient that you've both found humans who accept our true nature so readily," Solar observed with obvious suspicion. "While I alone maintain mission protocol."

"Your light emissions are hardly maintaining protocol," Lunar pointed out. "You've damaged electronics in two separate locations now that we know of."

Solar's skin temperature increased visibly. "At least I'm not lurking in food holding chambers with random Earth females."

"Enough," Eclipse interjected with predictable mediation. "We have suitable accommodations now. We should focus on the next phase of our mission."

"Finding mates," Solar stated. "Although it seems you two have already begun that process."

"I have no interest in mating with Poppy," Lunar lied automatically. The concept was absurd. His interaction with the human was purely investigative, regardless of her unusual compatibility with shadow frequencies. "Her perceptive abilities simply warrant investigation."

"And Rowan is merely facilitating our mission," Eclipse added unconvincingly.

Lunar couldn't help himself. "I think you're envious because you have not had a female show interest."

"I have an engagement tonight," Solar blustered. "At The Crash Zone."

"With whom?" Eclipse asked.

"A fire manipulator," Solar replied, "who demonstrates flame control techniques that may be useful for our understanding of Earth combat capabilities. If we are trapped here, we will need to defend ourselves."

"Her name?" Lunar asked, unable to resist highlighting Solar's hypocrisy.

Solar hesitated. "Dani Ember."

Lunar smirked.

"It's research," Solar insisted. "Unlike you two, I haven't forgotten why we're here."

Eclipse sighed. "Be careful. And try not to cause any more disturbances."

Solar turned away, effectively ending the conversation. Lunar retreated to explore his designated chamber undisturbed.

The room was acceptable with minimal windows, heavy coverings to block light, and sufficient space for proper shadow manipulation exercises. After securing the entry, Lunar removed the increasingly uncomfortable skin-suit, allowing his natural form to emerge. He placed the black tourmaline stone Poppy had given him on the sleeping platform.

His shadow-absorbing flesh immediately began processing the available darkness, replenishing energy reserves depleted by prolonged exposure to light. The relief was substantial. He moved through the space, testing shadow densities and identifying optimal positions for rest and regeneration.

Lunar retrieved the stone, allowing his senses to analyze its properties more thoroughly now that he could touch it with his unencumbered form.

The mineral absorbed ambient energy in patterns similar to his own biological processes, but at a much more primitive level. Still, its effectiveness was noteworthy. Combined with Poppy's unusual perceptive abilities, it suggested Earth might possess resources of value to the shadow territories.

. . .

PERSONAL LOG, *Supplemental:*

We have relocated to more suitable accommodations through the intervention of Eclipse's human contact, Rowan. The dwelling offers adequate separation between light and shadow zones, which should reduce conflict with Solar. However, the light-bearer continues to display aggression and territorial behavior typical of his kind.

More significantly, I have confirmed the human female Poppy possesses extraordinary perceptive abilities. She detected both my shadow-walking and Solar's light emissions without technological assistance. This suggests potential genetic variations in Earth species that were not included in our briefing materials.

Poppy has demonstrated knowledge of natural Earth minerals that interact with energy patterns. The black tourmaline she provided exhibits absorption properties that warrant further study. She has also referenced locations with deep shadows that may offer superior regeneration conditions.

I intend to continue observation of this anomalous human. Her abilities suggest possibilities beyond the simplistic mating objectives of our mission. The shadow territories could benefit from understanding how certain Earth beings perceive energy frequencies, potentially developing new concealment techniques against Solarus detection systems.

Eclipse and Solar both appear to be forming attachments to human females, despite their denials. This development may complicate mission parameters, but provides useful leverage if necessary.

For now, I will maintain the appearance of cooperation while pursuing independent objectives.

LUNAR COMPLETED his log entry and moved to the window, carefully avoiding direct light while observing the external environment. The desert landscape stretched before him, red rock formations creating complex shadow patterns as the sun moved across the sky.

In the distance, the town center was visible, where humans conducted their various activities. Many of them believed they were the only sentient life in their planetary system, a common delusion among developing species.

Yet Poppy had sensed him immediately. Had known he was different. Had offered assistance without fear or aggression.

There was something about her. He wanted to be

near her. Even now, he wanted to find her and pull her into the darkness with him.

Lunar returned to the room's darkest corner. The night would bring new opportunities for exploration, away from Solar's intrusive brightness and Eclipse's constant mediation.

Perhaps he would investigate these deep shadow locations Poppy had mentioned. Or perhaps he would observe the light-bearer's interaction with his fire manipulator at The Crash Zone to make sure he didn't draw trouble toward them. Either way, Earth was proving more interesting than anticipated.

The shadows had secrets to reveal. And Lunar had always been very, very good at discovering secrets.

5

NIGHT TRANSFORMED THE DESERT.

Poppy watched as the last ribbons of sunset faded from the western sky, leaving only the deepening blue that would soon give way to perfect darkness. She'd parked her old SUV at the end of a rugged dirt road, far enough from the light pollution of Duskrock that the stars would shine unfiltered. The scent of cooling earth and sage filled the air as she leaned against her vehicle, waiting.

She wasn't entirely sure he would come. She didn't give him directions, but something told her he could find her if he wanted to. Their connection at the retreat had been interrupted, and despite his acceptance of her invitation to explore the desert's nocturnal side, Lunar struck her as someone who might change his mind. Someone who kept his options open and his trust closely guarded.

The thought had barely formed when she felt it, that familiar cool presence, like a patch of shade on a hot day, moving toward her from the darkness beyond her headlights.

"You came," she said, smiling into the apparent emptiness.

"I said I would." Lunar's voice emerged from the shadows before his physical form did. He materialized like ink spreading through water. He wore the same restrictive skin-suit as earlier, but it seemed to have deteriorated, revealing glimpses of his true nature, a darkness deeper than the night itself. "The others are occupied with their own pursuits."

Poppy nodded, unsurprised. "Eclipse is having dinner with Rowan. And your sunshine friend is with Dani."

"You are well-informed for someone who claims to be uninvolved with our arrival." Suspicion colored his voice.

"Duskrock is a small town. People talk." She pushed off from her vehicle. "And I pay attention."

The desert stretched around them, red rocks transformed to purple-black silhouettes against the darkening sky. Twisted juniper trees cast strange shadows in the fading light, their gnarled forms like ancient sentinels guarding the wilderness.

"I brought you something," Poppy said, reaching into her bag. She handed him a metal container. "More black tourmaline. Different formations. I thought you might want to test which ones work best."

Lunar accepted the container, his fingers brushing hers in the exchange. Even that brief contact sent a cool ripple along her skin, like dipping her hand into a night-chilled stream.

"Your perception of my needs is unusually accurate," he observed.

"I told you. I work with nocturnal creatures. I understand the need for darkness." She gestured toward the trail leading away from the vehicle. "Shall we? I want to show you something."

Lunar fell into step beside her as they moved away from the car. Poppy clicked on a small red-filtered flashlight, providing just enough illumination to navigate the trail without disrupting their night vision.

"The red light doesn't disturb most desert animals," she explained. "It lets us see without being seen."

"A principle familiar to shadow-dwellers," Lunar

noted. His eyes began to glow with red beams, mimicking her flashlight. "Observation without detection."

They walked in comfortable silence, their footsteps muffled by the sandy soil. The trail wound between massive boulders and through stands of prickly pear cactus, their flat pads like outstretched hands in the darkness.

"The desert seems dead to most people who only see it during the day," Poppy said after a while. "But at night, it's full of life. Kangaroo rats, kit foxes, owls, bats, all moving through the darkness, sensing what humans can't."

As if summoned by her words, a great horned owl swept silently overhead, its wingspan impressive against the star-filled sky. Lunar tracked its movement with remarkable precision.

"Your night vision is excellent," Poppy observed.

"My species evolved in perpetual darkness," Lunar replied. "Light is the abnormality for us."

They continued up the trail as it climbed toward a ridge. The temperature dropped noticeably, the day's heat surrendering to the embrace of night. Around them, the desert awakened, the soft rustling of packrats in the underbrush, the distant yip of coyotes, the whispering passage of a hunting bat.

"We're almost there," Poppy said, pointing toward a dark opening in the rockface ahead. "Cave entrances like this one are scattered throughout the area. Most tourists never find them."

The cave mouth was little more than a crack in the red sandstone, easily overlooked unless you knew where to search. Poppy slipped through the narrow opening. Lunar followed gracefully. Inside, the passage widened, opening into a chamber large enough to stand in comfortably.

"This was a seasonal shelter for indigenous people hundreds of years ago," Poppy explained, her voice echoing slightly in the enclosed space. "There are pictographs further in, but that's not what I wanted to show you."

She led him deeper into the cave, where the passage narrowed again before opening into a second, larger chamber. Here, she switched off her flashlight, plunging them into absolute darkness. His eyes also stopped shining their red lights.

"Wait," she said softly. "Let your eyes adjust."

They stood in perfect stillness. Gradually, impossibly, the darkness began to lighten. Soft blue-green points of light appeared on the ceiling and walls, like earthbound stars.

"Bioluminescent fungi," Poppy explained, her

voice hushed with reverence. "They grow in only a few caves in this region. They need complete darkness to thrive, but they create their own light."

The delicate glow cast just enough illumination to reveal the contours of the cave and the silhouette of her companion. In this light, Lunar seemed more at ease, his form less rigid than it had been outside.

"Light born from darkness," he murmured. "A paradox."

"I thought you might appreciate it," Poppy said. "It reminded me of you, somehow."

Lunar turned toward her, his eyes reflecting the subtle glow of the fungi. "You continue to perceive aspects of my nature that should be imperceptible to humans."

"I've always seen things others miss." Poppy moved toward the center of the chamber, where a natural depression in the floor formed a kind of bench. She sat, patting the space beside her. "My grandmother was the same way. She called it having the sight."

Lunar hesitated before joining her, maintaining a careful distance. "On my world, such perception would be valued. The shadow territories reward those who can detect subtle energies."

"Shadow territories," Poppy repeated. "Tell me about your home."

For a moment, she thought he might refuse, but then he began to speak, his voice taking on a rhythmic quality, like the sound of flowing water over stones.

"Zorveya is tidal-locked, one side in perpetual day, one in eternal night. The Lunaris Zone exists in darkness, our cities built in the shadows of mountains and deep canyons. We have evolved to process energy differently from those of the light."

"And the others? Solar and Eclipse?"

"Solar is of the Solarus Zone, where light never fades. His kind absorbs and channels solar radiation as we absorb and channel darkness. Eclipse is of the Twilight Belt, the narrow band between our worlds. His people are mediators by nature. They keep the peace between the dark and light."

Poppy listened, fascinated by the idea of a world divided by such differences. "And you're here to prove your people can coexist?"

Lunar's expression shifted subtly. "That is the official mission. A diplomatic experiment."

"But you have your own agenda," she guessed.

His gaze sharpened. "You are unusually perceptive."

"I'm good at reading people. Even alien people, apparently." She smiled, then grew serious. "Whatever your real reason for being here, I'm glad you came. I've always felt different, as if I were tuned to a frequency no one else could hear. Meeting you confirms that I'm not crazy."

The soft glow of the fungi seemed to pulse gently, as if responding to her words. In this intimate light, Poppy could see more details of Lunar's true nature beneath the deteriorating skin-suit, patterns of darkness that flowed and shifted like liquid shadow.

"Your skin is falling apart," she observed. "Like Solar's was earlier."

Lunar touched the membrane at his neck, where it had begun to separate from his actual form. "The materials were not designed for prolonged use. Earth's atmosphere accelerates the degradation."

"You could take it off," Poppy suggested. "If it's uncomfortable. I don't mind."

He studied her for a long moment, seeming to assess her sincerity. "We were warned that our true forms may be disturbing to human perception."

"Try me," she challenged gently.

After another moment of hesitation, Lunar reached behind his neck. There was a soft hissing sound as he released some hidden mechanism, and the skin-suit began to peel away, falling from his body like a shed snake skin. He took his human clothes off to peel out of the membrane.

Poppy watched in fascination as his form was revealed. Where Solar was a being of pure light, Lunar was composed of what seemed to be living shadow. His body maintained a humanoid shape, but his skin absorbed rather than reflected light, creating a silhouette of perfect darkness outlined by the subtle glow of the fungi. Within that darkness, patterns moved like stars seen through deep space, tiny points of light swirling in cosmic patterns.

She looked down. How could she not? Here was a naked alien. But it was too dark for her to make out any distinct shapes.

"You're beautiful," she whispered, genuinely awed.

Lunar looked surprised, the expression visible in the subtle shift of the star-like patterns within his form. "That is not the typical reaction."

"I've never been typical," Poppy replied with a small smile. "May I..." she hesitated, hand half-raised toward him.

"You wish to touch me?" He sounded genuinely confused by the request.

"If that's okay."

"It is not dangerous, as Solar's energy might be," Lunar said after a moment. "But it will feel unusual."

Poppy reached out slowly, giving him time to withdraw if he changed his mind. Her fingers made contact with his arm, and she gasped softly at the sensation. His skin was cool but not cold, with a strange texture like velvet darkness. Where she touched him, the star-like patterns within his form swirled toward her fingers, as if drawn to her warmth.

"I feel it," she whispered. "Your energy. It's like... like the moment before rain falls, or the instant after a candle is extinguished and smoke twirls up into the air."

Lunar remained perfectly still beneath her touch, but she could feel a subtle tremor running through him. "Your insight is accurate. Few beings outside my kind have ever described the sensation so precisely."

Emboldened, Poppy let her hand trail up his arm to his shoulder. The patterns followed her touch, leaving luminous trails in their wake that slowly faded back to darkness. The sensation was mesmerizing, creating a feedback loop of energy between them.

"You conduct shadow frequencies," Lunar observed, his voice dropping lower. "This is unexpected."

"Is that good or bad?" Poppy asked.

Lunar's hand moved to cover hers, pressing her palm more firmly against his chest. The contact heightened the sensation, sending cool shivers of energy up her arm. It didn't feel like touching a human. It was more like shoving her hand into a ghost, sensing the supernatural essence flowing around her.

"Very good," he murmured, his voice resonating in a way that seemed to bypass her ears to vibrate directly against her bones.

Poppy felt her breath quicken, her body reacting to his closeness in unexpected ways. The energy transfer between them felt deeply personal, more intimate than any physical contact she had known before.

"What do I feel like to you?" she asked.

"Like finding darkness after too much light," Lunar answered. "A relief. A sanctuary." His hand moved to her face, fingers tracing the curve of her cheek with unexpected gentleness. "You absorb and reflect shadow energy in patterns I have only observed in my own kind. It creates a resonance."

The bioluminescent fungi appeared to fade in response to his words, as if the darkness separating them was absorbing the light. In the growing shadows, Poppy's other senses became sharper. She concentrated on the gentle sound of their breathing, the cool sensation of his skin touching hers, and the subtle aroma of desert sage lingering on her clothes.

"We were given basic instructions for this situation," he whispered.

When his lips found hers, the kiss was gentle, like drinking water from a night-chilled spring. Poppy leaned into it, her hands finding purchase on his shoulders. The star-patterns within his form swirled faster, creating eddies of light and darkness that reflected in the chamber around them.

"But you were not in the mission parameters," Lunar said when they finally broke apart.

Poppy laughed softly. "I would hope not."

"My purpose here is complex," he continued, his expression serious. "There are objectives beyond what Eclipse and Solar understand."

"You have secrets," Poppy acknowledged. "So do I."

"Yet you trust me," Lunar observed, sounding genuinely puzzled.

"I trust what I feel," she corrected. "And what I feel with you is right. Like finding a piece that's been missing."

Something shifted in his expression at her words. His hands framed her face.

"Show me more," he requested, his voice barely above a whisper.

Poppy didn't need to ask what he meant. She drew him closer, her lips meeting his again with greater urgency. This time, the kiss deepened, and she felt the energy of his true nature flow over her skin like water. It was exhilarating, each point of contact between them creating tiny whirlpools of sensation that traveled through her nervous system.

With deliberate movements, she slipped her jacket from her shoulders, then pulled her shirt over her head. The cool air of the cave raised goosebumps on her exposed skin, but they were nothing compared to the ripples of energy that flowed from Lunar's touch as his hands traced the contours of her body.

"Your warmth," he murmured against her throat. "It creates patterns I have never observed."

Poppy shivered, not from cold but from the intensity of sensation. "Good patterns?"

"Fascinating patterns," he clarified, his fingers exploring the curve of her waist with a scientific precision that was rapidly giving way to something more primal.

The bioluminescent fungi responded to their energy exchange, dimming and brightening in waves that matched the rhythm of their movements. Poppy guided Lunar's hands to her breasts, gasping at the vibration that traveled from his fingertips into her belly.

"You respond to shadow energy," Lunar observed, his voice deepening with what might have been wonder.

"I've always been drawn to darkness," Poppy admitted, her voice catching as his thumbs traced circles on her sensitive skin.

Lunar's eyes, now visible as slightly brighter patterns within his shadowed face, studied her with intense focus. "You are an anomaly, Poppy Jensen. A singularity."

She smiled at the unusual compliment, as her hands began to explore his body. His physique was both solid and fluid, with the lines between his energy and the darkness around him blurring as her fingers traced patterns on his chest.

Poppy pushed her pants down her legs to strip completely. Her hips bumped into his, not feeling the telltale sign of arousal she was used to with men. Instead, the space between his hips was flat. She looked up at him. "I'm not sure how we're supposed to, you know, fit together."

"I assure you we are compatible," he answered.

Together, they sank onto the stone floor of the cave, now softened by Poppy's discarded jacket.

Lunar's touch was exploratory and methodical, as he studied her body with the care of a scientist uncovering a new world. Yet there was something more than curiosity in his movements. There was a hunger, a need that transcended physical desire. When his fingers traced her skin, energy followed, creating pathways of pleasure.

"The patterns," he murmured, watching her reactions with undisguised fascination. "They flow through you, connecting us."

Poppy could see it too. Where their skin met, the darkness of his form seemed to flow into her, creating swirls of shadow that danced across her body before fading. It was beautiful and strange, intimate in a way that went beyond the physical.

When he finally moved above her, his body aligned with hers, Poppy felt as if the night sky collapsed upon them. The ache inside her was deep. Her thighs parted. Their connection was instant, with energy streaming from him to her, forming a circuit that grew stronger with every movement.

"I can feel you," she whispered, her hands gripping his shoulders. "Everywhere."

She arched her hips into him, searching for more. His body seemed to shift and change. The tingling pushed deep inside her, vibrating as a cock formed to fit her perfectly. The stretch became almost painful, but she was helpless to stop it. He pulsed more than thrust, undulating himself inside her sex.

The sensation was unlike anything she had ever experienced. Pleasure originated not just where their bodies joined, but everywhere his energy touched hers. It spread through her in waves, cool fire that built with each careful thrust.

Lunar's gaze never left her face as he watched the effect of their connection. The star-patterns within his form accelerated, swirling faster as his composure began to slip. Darkness gathered around them, the fungi dimming until only the faintest outline of their bodies remained visible.

Poppy's other senses heightened dramatically. The sound of their breathing, the slide of his body against hers, the subtle vibrations of energy that passed between them, all became more intense, more immediate.

"I cannot maintain control of the shadows,"

Lunar warned, his voice strained. "They respond to your energy."

"Let them," Poppy urged, pulling him closer. "I'm not afraid of the dark."

The shadows responded to her acceptance, swirling around them like living ink, enveloping them in perfect darkness. Within this void, their connection deepened, the boundaries between their bodies blurring as shadow energy flowed freely between them.

Poppy surrendered to the sensation, letting the waves of pleasure carry her higher. She felt herself becoming part of his darkness, her consciousness expanding beyond the physical. Each movement of their bodies created ripples in the shadow energy that surrounded them, amplifying sensations until they bordered on overwhelming.

Lunar's control slipped further as his rhythm intensified. The star-patterns within his form began to pulse in time with their movements, creating brief flashes of illumination that captured moments of their union like cosmic photographs.

Words became unnecessary. They communicated through touch and energy, each response guiding the next movement. Poppy felt herself approaching the edge of something profound, a pleasure so intense it transcended anything she'd ever known. She gripped Lunar's shoulders, anchoring herself.

When release finally claimed her, it was like floating into the night sky. Pleasure expanded outward in ripples of shadow energy that merged with Lunar's own. Lunar followed her into that shared oblivion, his form momentarily losing cohesion as his own climax overtook him. For a moment that seemed to stretch into eternity, they were completely intertwined, and it was impossible to distinguish where one ended and the other began.

Slowly, reality reasserted itself. The shadows receded, returning to their natural state as Lunar regained control of his energy. The fungi glowed softly once more to reveal their entwined forms on the cave floor.

Poppy lay beneath him, breathless and amazed. Her skin tingled with residual energy, tiny patterns of shadow still swirling across the surface before gradually fading. She felt changed in some way, as if the experience had altered something fundamental within her.

"That was," she began, searching for words that could possibly describe what had happened.

"Unexpected," Lunar supplied, his expression a

mixture of wonder and concern. He moved to her side, his form still mostly shadow but more defined now. The star-patterns within him were calmer.

"Beautiful," she corrected, turning to face him. "I've never experienced anything like that."

"Nor have I," Lunar admitted. He studied her curiously, reaching out to trace a lingering shadow pattern on her shoulder. "Your body has temporarily retained some of my energy signature. This should not be possible for a human."

"Maybe I'm not as human as you think," Poppy suggested with a small smile.

"Perhaps not," he agreed, more seriously than she had intended. "The resonance between us is unprecedented in my experience. It warrants further investigation."

Poppy chuckled softly at his clinical description of what had just occurred between them. "Is that your way of saying you want to see me again?"

Lunar seemed to consider this, his expression thoughtful. "I find myself drawn to you in ways that contradict my mission objectives. This is problematic."

"Because connecting with an Earth female is exactly what you're supposed to be doing?" Poppy pointed out.

"The connection itself is not problematic. It is the nature and intensity of it that complicates matters." His fingers continued to trace patterns on her skin, as if he couldn't quite stop touching her. "I have responsibilities beyond what Eclipse and Solar understand."

Poppy propped herself up on one elbow, studying his shadowed face. "You're not just here for this diplomatic experiment, are you?"

"No," Lunar admitted. "My role is more complex."

"Are you going to tell me what it is?"

"Not yet." His hand moved to cup her face. "The less you know, the safer you remain."

Poppy should have been alarmed by this admission, but something within her trusted him despite his secrets. "I'm pretty good at taking care of myself."

"I believe that," Lunar said. "Your affinity for shadow energy and your perceptive abilities suggest unusual resilience. Nevertheless, caution is warranted."

Outside the cave, a coyote howled, its voice carrying through the desert night. Poppy listened to the sound, reminded of the world beyond their intimate sanctuary.

"We should probably head back soon," she said reluctantly. "Desert nights get cold."

"I am not affected by temperature variations,"

Lunar stated, then added with what might have been humor, "but I understand humans require more consistent thermal conditions."

Poppy smiled at his clinical manner of expressing concern. She sat up, gathering her scattered clothing in the dim light. As she dressed, she could feel Lunar watching her, his gaze almost tangible in the darkness.

"Your shadow stones," Lunar said suddenly, retrieving the metal container she had given him earlier. He opened it, examining the different specimens of black tourmaline within. "They absorb energy in a pattern similar to my own biological processes. How did you know?"

"I didn't, not consciously," Poppy admitted, pulling her shirt over her head. "I've always been drawn to certain stones, certain places. It's like they speak to me, in a way I can't quite explain. I just know things. Instinctively."

Lunar selected one of the larger specimens, a raw tourmaline crystal with complex facets. "This one resonates most strongly with my energy signature. May I keep it?"

"Of course. They're all for you." She watched as he held the stone, noting how the darkness of his form seemed to flow into and around it.

Lunar retrieved his skin-suit, examining it with obvious distaste. "The membrane continues to deteriorate. Soon it will be non-functional."

"Do you really need it?" Poppy asked. "I mean, in the dark, no one would notice the difference anyway."

"In darkness, no," Lunar agreed. "But I cannot remain permanently in shadow. The mission requires interaction with the human population in various settings."

With obvious reluctance, he began to reapply the skin-suit, his true form gradually disappearing beneath the constraining membrane. Poppy watched with a twinge of sadness, already missing the beauty of his natural state.

When they were both dressed and ready to leave, Lunar paused at the entrance to the chamber, looking back at the bioluminescent fungi.

"This place," he said quietly, "it reminds me of the shadow gardens in the deep canyons of my home. Places of beauty born from darkness."

"We can come back," Poppy promised. "There are other caves, other hidden places in the desert. I could show you."

Lunar nodded, a simple gesture that somehow conveyed more meaning than words could express.

He reached for her hand, his fingers twining with hers as they made their way back through the narrow passage toward the cave entrance.

Outside, the desert night greeted them with a blanket of stars. The air had cooled considerably, but Poppy barely noticed, still warmed by the memory of their connection. They walked in comfortable silence back toward her vehicle, the red-filtered flashlight casting just enough light to navigate the trail.

"The others cannot know of this," Lunar said as they approached the SUV. "Not yet. Eclipse would see it as a distraction from the mission. Solar would ask questions I am not prepared to answer."

"Your secret is safe with me," Poppy assured him. "I'm pretty good at keeping things to myself."

Lunar studied her face in the starlight, his expression unreadable. "I believe you are. Perhaps that is another reason we resonate so strongly."

He reached up to touch her face one last time, his fingers cool against her skin. "Until we meet again, Poppy Jensen. Watch for me in the shadows."

Before she could respond, he stepped back, merging with the darkness so completely that she couldn't tell exactly when he disappeared. One moment he was there, the next only night remained.

Poppy stood for a long moment, staring into the

darkness where he had been. The desert night surrounded her, alive with subtle sounds and movements, a world most humans never truly saw. She belonged to that world now more than ever, connected to its shadows in ways she was only beginning to understand.

As she climbed into her vehicle and started the engine, Poppy smiled to herself. She had always been drawn to darkness, to the mysteries that lived in shadow. Tonight, for the first time, the darkness had reached back.

And it had changed her forever.

6

LUNAR SENSED THE APPROACHING VEHICLES
before Poppy did.

In the predawn darkness, he had been watching
her sleep, fascinated by the human cycle of
consciousness and the peaceful vulnerability it represented. Her breathing remained deep and even, her
mind temporarily disconnected from awareness
while her body performed essential metabolic
functions.

From his position outside the window of her
small cottage, Lunar monitored the surrounding
desert landscape. Night creatures moved through the
brush, their energy patterns distinct and purposeful.
An owl glided silently over the property, hunting. A

fox slipped between cactus formations, its presence barely disturbing the ambient energy field.

He meant only to watch over her as he absorbed the darkness. Then something changed. Three vehicles approached along the distant access road, their mechanical vibrations creating discordant patterns in the night. Lunar focused his senses, analyzing the disruption. Not typical tourist transport. Not retreat staff. The vehicles moved with coordinated precision, maintaining exact distances from each other, slowing at strategic intervals to minimize noise.

Hunters.

Lunar slipped along the shadows into her home. He moved to Poppy's bedside, flowing across the room without sound. He placed his hand on her shoulder, applying light pressure. Her eyes opened immediately, awareness returning with surprising speed for a human.

"Lunar? How did you get in...?" She became instantly alert. "Someone's coming."

Lunar nodded. "Three vehicles. Coordinated approach pattern."

Poppy got out of bed and moved to the window. She grabbed a pair of binoculars and peered through the gap in the curtains, her body tense. "Black SUVs. Tinted windows. That's weird. Government or private security? They shouldn't be out here. There's nothing but—*no, wait.* The side says Milano Enterprises."

"Milano?" Lunar studied Poppy's worried expression. "Who are they?"

"They're the parent company to the Milano Foundation," Poppy said, her voice hardening slightly. "They claim to fund wildlife conservation and medical research, but there have always been rumors surrounding their test facilities in the desert. I have friends who have tried to track their funds. Very little of the funding makes it to actual conservation projects. Then there are the strange lights, unusual security, and people who asked too many questions who suddenly disappeared. What the hell are they doing out here?"

Lunar couldn't say, but it looked like they were coming toward them.

"I don't like this." She lowered the binoculars and looked at him. "If rumors of them hold true, there is only one reason I can think of that such a company would be coming here. To catch an alien."

"I will leave. I do not wish to put you in danger," Lunar stated. He intended to slip back into the night and watch over her from a distance. If he had to, he'd lead them away from her.

"Don't you dare try to leave without me," Poppy ordered, already moving around the room gathering essentials. Her efficiency impressed him. "This doesn't make sense. How did they find you?"

"Unknown," Lunar replied.

"Let's not find out. We need to go," Poppy said, pulling on dark clothing. "They're still at the access road, but that only gives us minutes."

Lunar assessed their tactical options. The approaching vehicles blocked the primary escape route. His shadow-walking abilities would allow him to evade capture, but Poppy lacked this capability. He could try to carry her with him, but that was new territory, and he wasn't sure how that would affect her biology. Sharing energy was one thing. Transforming her into his energy, another entirely.

"There is an alternative exit?" he asked.

"Back trail through the wash," Poppy confirmed, stuffing items into a small backpack. "It's rough terrain, but it connects to the cave system I showed you. If we can reach it, we can disappear."

Lunar removed his skin-suit and shoved the deteriorating membrane into a pack. In darkness, his true form would provide superior camouflage. "Time is limited. Take only essentials."

Poppy nodded, grabbing water bottles and what

appeared to be energy-dense food bars. She added a small medical kit and her flashlight with the red filter. "Ready."

They slipped out the back door into the desert night. Lunar could hear the vehicles, engines quieting as they approached the final stretch to the cottage. Poppy led him to a dry streambed running through the property, with its banks offering cover.

"Stay close," Poppy whispered, leading him along the sandy bottom of the wash. "The footing is treacherous."

Lunar wasn't worried. He could easily drift over the ground as he followed her. Though clearly limited by her human body, he was impressed by her night navigation skills. Their bond from the night before appeared to have grown stronger, enabling a silent cooperation that improved their chances of escaping. She moved with practiced efficiency, avoiding obstacles without hesitation.

Behind them, vehicle doors opened and closed. Voices carried on the still night air. They appeared to be too distant for Poppy to hear, but they were clear to Lunar's enhanced senses.

"Property appears vacant. Heat signatures were detected within the structure approximately ten minutes ago. Subjects may have fled."

"Establish perimeter. Prepare for a sweep with electromagnetic sensors. Subjects cannot have gone far."

Electromagnetic sensors. The device they referenced was unfamiliar but concerning. He did not recall it from the Galaxy Alien Mail Order Brides' information packets. If these humans possessed technology capable of detecting his energy signature, simple physical concealment would prove inadequate.

"We must increase distance," Lunar informed Poppy quietly. "They have detection equipment."

Poppy nodded, not questioning how he knew that. She picked up her pace as they followed the winding wash deeper into the desert. The red rock formations loomed around them, creating complex shadow patterns in the fading night. Dawn approached, bringing increased vulnerability for Lunar's shadow form.

After twenty minutes of rapid movement, the wash intersected with a narrow canyon. Poppy led him up a nearly invisible path that switchbacked up the canyon wall. From this elevation, Lunar could see the cottage in the distance. Figures with handheld devices moved in search patterns around the prop-

erty, their methodical coverage suggesting profes-
sional training.

"The cave entrance is just ahead," Poppy said, her
breathing controlled despite the exertion. "Once we're
inside, we'll be harder to track. The rock composition
interferes with most scanning technologics."

The cave entrance was concealed behind a rock
outcropping, invisible unless one knew exactly where
to look. Poppy moved a carefully arranged pile of
stones that had appeared natural but actually marked
the low entrance. Lunar slipped in first. Beyond lay
darkness deeper than the night outside, a perfect
environment for Lunar's abilities.

Once inside, Poppy pulled the stones back to
hide the entrance and activated her red-filtered light,
revealing a narrow passage that descended into the
earth. "Watch your head. It gets tight in places."

They moved deeper into the cave system, the
temperature dropping noticeably as they left the
surface world behind. The passages twisted and
branched, forming a natural labyrinth that Poppy
navigated with confidence.

"How do you know this system so well?" Lunar
asked as they passed through a particularly narrow
section.

"I map caves as a hobby," Poppy explained. "Most tourists and even locals don't know these exist. The indigenous people used them for storage and ceremonies, but kept their locations secret."

After several minutes of descent, the passage opened into a larger chamber. Unlike the cave they had visited the previous night, this one contained no bioluminescent fungi. The darkness was absolute except for Poppy's small red light.

"We should be safe here for now," Poppy said, setting down her pack. "This chamber isn't on any official maps, and it's deep enough that standard scanning equipment can't penetrate."

Lunar released his full shadow form, no longer constrained by the need for partial human appearance. His energy expanded into the darkness, merging with and enhancing it. The chamber's natural shadows welcomed him, creating a perfect environment for energy regeneration.

"Your true form," Poppy observed, watching as the star-like patterns within his shadow body became more pronounced in the perfect darkness. "It's even more beautiful here."

"This environment is optimal," Lunar confirmed. "The cave's natural energy patterns complement my own."

Poppy sat on a smooth rock formation, her expression thoughtful in the dim red light. "Those men, they're looking for you specifically, aren't they? Not just investigating strange occurrences. How else would they know to come looking at my house?"

"Yes," Lunar said. "Their search patterns and equipment suggest prior knowledge of extraterrestrial energy signatures. We must contact Eclipse and Solar. They may also be targeted."

Poppy pulled out her communication device, examining it with a frown. "No signal down here. We'd have to get closer to the surface."

"Unacceptable risk during daylight while we are being followed," Lunar decided. "We will attempt communication after sunset."

Poppy nodded, accepting his assessment without argument. "So we wait."

"Yes."

She arranged her pack as a makeshift pillow and stretched out on a relatively flat section of the cave floor. "Might as well rest, then. It's going to be a long day."

Lunar watched as she made herself comfortable despite the harsh environment. Her adaptability continued to impress him. Most beings would exhibit stress responses to sudden evacuation and hiding in a cave, yet Poppy showed only acceptance of their circumstances.

"You are unusually calm in this situation," he observed.

Poppy smiled slightly. "I work with injured predators, remember? Staying calm in tense situations is a survival skill."

"A valuable capability," Lunar acknowledged.

"Besides," she added, "I've spent my life feeling like I don't quite fit in the normal world. Finding out aliens exist and connecting with one seems weirdly right, even with the shady corporation chasing us part."

Lunar considered this perspective. "You identify more with the unknown than the familiar."

"Pretty much," Poppy agreed. "Normal never worked for me."

Her acceptance of their situation, of him, created unfamiliar response patterns in Lunar's energy field. Throughout his existence, he had been defined by opposition, shadow against light, stealth against exposure, isolation against connection. Poppy's ready acceptance of his true nature represented a paradigm he had not encountered before.

"You should rest," he advised. "I will maintain vigilance."

Poppy studied him for a moment, then patted the space beside her. "Come sit by me, at least. That way I know you're not just a really vivid dream I'm going to wake up from."

Lunar hesitated briefly before moving to join her. As he settled beside her, she turned on her side and reached for his hand, her fingers intertwining with his shadow form. The connection sent ripples through his energy field, pleasant vibrations that intensified where their bodies touched.

"What were you doing at my house? I thought you had gone back to your friends," she said, her voice soft in the darkness.

"I followed you and was watching you through your window."

She gave a small laugh. "Next time, just come home with me. Don't disappear into the night."

"I needed to rejuvenate," he said. "And to think about your body's response to mine."

"I'll accept that. Can you tell me about your world?" Poppy stared up into the darkness. "What's it like to live in eternal night?"

"The Lunaris Zone looks much like this cave," Lunar explained, finding himself unusually willing to share information about his home. "Our cities are built in deep canyons and cave systems, protected from the rare light that might reflect from the Twilight Belt."

"So your people evolved to thrive in darkness," Poppy mused. "Like nocturnal animals here on Earth."

"A simplified comparison, but essentially correct," Lunar confirmed. "We process energy in forms beyond the visible spectrum. We perceive heat differentials, magnetic fluctuations, and shadow densities that light-dependent species cannot detect."

"And the star patterns within you?" Poppy asked, her fingers lightly tracing one such constellation on his arm. "What are those?"

"Energy nexus points," Lunar explained, suppressing a pleasurable shiver at her touch. "Locations where cosmic radiation is processed and channeled throughout my form. The patterns are unique to each individual, like your human fingerprints."

"They're beautiful," Poppy said simply.

They lapsed into comfortable silence, Poppy's head eventually resting against his leg as fatigue overcame her. Lunar remained alert, monitoring the cave system for any sign of intrusion while allowing part of his consciousness to enjoy the simple contact between them.

7

Hours passed in the timeless darkness of the cave. The vibrations from above told Lunar that Milano's forces had expanded their search pattern. They were deploying throughout the canyons and ridges in a systematic grid, closing in on their location. Occasionally, Lunar detected faint vibrations from the surface world, vehicles passing on distant roads, the movement of larger wildlife, and the subtle shift of temperature as the morning approached the afternoon. None indicated an immediate threat to their specific hiding place.

Despite the circumstances that had brought them here, Lunar found the isolation with Poppy unexpectedly satisfying. In the Lunaris Zone, proximity to others was carefully regulated, interactions governed by strict protocols of necessity and purpose. Casual contact was rare, sustained physical connection rarer still. Yet here in this Earth cave, the simple act of sitting beside Poppy while she slept created harmonies in his energy field that he had never experienced in his home environment.

Eventually, Poppy stirred, consciousness returning as she lifted her head from beside his leg. "How long was I asleep?"

"Approximately eight Earth hours," Lunar informed her. "It is late afternoon on the surface."

"Eight hours? Damn. I must have slipped into a coma." Poppy stretched, her body moving with the grace he had come to appreciate.

"I cannot say. I am unfamiliar with the energy signature of a coma," he said.

She chuckled. "I just meant I must have been more tired than I realized to sleep like that with all that is going on."

"That would be from our energy exchange. I also had to rejuvenate after." Lunar didn't add that a human's rejuvenation process was much less efficient.

"Any sign of trouble?" she asked.

"Milano's forces expanded their search grid

above," Lunar reported. "They're deploying vehicles and personnel throughout the canyon system."

"They'll be watching the cottage," Poppy said thoughtfully, "and they'll probably have people stationed at the main access points to the area too."

"A standard containment strategy," Lunar agreed. "They are attempting to restrict our movement options until we are forced to surface."

"Good thing I know all the non-standard exits," Poppy replied with a small smile. She reached for her pack, extracting water and food bars. "Here. I don't know if you need this stuff, but human hospitality dictates I offer."

Lunar accepted the items, finding the concept of hospitality in a crisis situation intriguing. He gave them back to her. "I can process these materials for energy, though less efficiently than shadow absorption. You should keep the supplies for yourself."

She quickly ate in silence.

"I know it's still daylight out there, but we should be able to reach a section of the cave where I can get cell reception," Poppy said, repacking her supplies. "We can contact your friends and figure out the next steps. I don't like the idea of them being hunted."

"A logical approach," Lunar agreed. "But they will know if they are hunted. Just as I did."

Poppy nodded, her expression turning more serious. "What exactly is your mission here, Lunar? And don't tell me again that it's finding compatible humans to prove peaceful coexistence. You already told me there is more to it."

The direct question activated Lunar's security protocols. Information compartmentalization was a standard procedure for shadow operatives. However, he felt an unusual urge to be more transparent with Poppy. Her loyalty and their developing bond built trust that surpassed usual caution.

"You are correct," he acknowledged. "My assigned role extends beyond the stated diplomatic mission."

"What's the real purpose?"

"Intelligence gathering," Lunar revealed. "While Eclipse and Solar promote the official narrative of peaceful cultural exchange, I was tasked with assessing Earth's strategic value and potential threat level."

"You're a spy," Poppy translated.

"Shadow Intelligence operative," Lunar corrected. "Though your term is essentially accurate."

Poppy considered this revelation, her expression thoughtful rather than alarmed. "So your people are what, considering Earth for colonization? Resource extraction? Military purposes?"

"All possibilities requiring evaluation," Lunar confirmed. "The shadow territories of Zorveya face resource limitations after centuries of inequitable distribution. New worlds with compatible environments represent potential solutions. If war breaks out on my homeworld, the light-dwellers would be at an advantage as they have the majority of the planetary resources."

"You can't just feed on darkness?" she asked.

"For a time, but there are other considerations necessary on my planet. When we reproduce, children are unable to process the darkness or light fully. They live in the twilight and consume meals much like you do until they are twelve years old. At that time, they adapt to their zone.

"They'll starve your children? They'd do that?" Poppy frowned.

He didn't answer. War was a dirty business.

"Do you," she bit her lip, "have children?"

"I have not reproduced."

"Can we...? I mean, should I be like on something?" she stammered. "Birth control, I mean."

"It is not necessary. If I decide to have a child, I would discuss the energy transfer with you. It takes a long time to gestate. Approximately one full Earth week."

"Human babies take nine months."

He grimaced. "That sounds unpleasant."

Poppy was silent for a moment, processing this information. "So what have you decided? About Earth, I mean. Are we a viable target?"

The question carried personal implications beyond strategic assessment. Lunar recognized the underlying concern in her voice, the unasked question about her own world's safety.

"My assessment remains incomplete," he said carefully. "Earth presents both valuable resources and significant complications. Its technological development level is inconsistent, advanced in some areas while primitive in others. Its political fragmentation creates strategic vulnerabilities but also complicates potential engagement."

"That's the official report," Poppy observed. "What's your personal opinion?"

Lunar had not anticipated this distinction. Shadow operatives were not encouraged to maintain personal perspectives separate from mission objectives. Yet his experience on Earth, particularly his connection with Poppy, had created precisely such a division.

"I find Earth unexpectedly valuable," he admitted. "Not merely for its physical resources, but for aspects of existence I had not previously encountered."

"Like what?" Poppy pressed.

"Freedom from rigid structures. Adaptation to constant change. Connection without strategic purpose." Lunar's gaze met hers in the dim red light. "You."

The simple acknowledgment hung between them in the darkness. Poppy's energy field shifted in response, creating harmonic patterns that resonated with his own shadow essence.

"That's quite a confession from a shadow spy," she said.

"It is unauthorized," Lunar acknowledged. "My superiors would consider such personal valuation a mission compromise."

"Am I?" Poppy asked. "Compromising your mission, I mean."

Lunar considered the question. "Yes. My experience with you has changed my perspective. I now hold viewpoints that conflict with my assigned purpose."

"So what will you do?" Poppy's question was direct, her gaze unwavering.

Before Lunar could respond, a subtle vibration traveled through the cave system. He stiffened, his shadow senses expanding outward to analyze the disturbance.

"What is it?" Poppy asked, noting his changed demeanor.

"Movement at the upper cave entrance," Lunar replied, his voice lowered. "Multiple entities. Controlled descent patterns."

Poppy's expression hardened. "They found us?"

"Not yet," Lunar corrected. "They are searching methodically, but have not located the path to this specific chamber."

"That phone call will have to wait. We need to move deeper," Poppy decided. "There's another level below this one, with underwater passages that connect to a different cave system."

Lunar processed this information against his mental mapping of their surroundings. "The vibration patterns suggest at least six individuals with equipment. Their search grid is systematic."

"They must have better scanning tech than I thought," Poppy muttered, securing her pack. "The rock composition should have blocked most conventional signals."

"We are not the first to visit this place. They may possess technology derived from previous extraterrestrial encounters." Lunar followed her toward a narrow fissure at the back of the chamber. "Including shadow detection capabilities."

The passageway Poppy led him through narrowed until she had to turn sideways to progress, the rough stone walls pressing close on either side. For beings who valued open space, such confinement could create panic. For a shadow-dweller like Lunar, the tight darkness was almost comforting, reminiscent of the security tunnels that connected Lunaris settlements.

"Watch your step here," Poppy warned, her voice barely above a whisper. "There's a drop."

Her concern was endearing.

The passage opened suddenly into vertical space, a natural chimney descending into deeper darkness. Poppy directed her red light downward, revealing a ten-meter drop to a lower level. Handholds had been carved into the stone wall, ancient and worn but still functional.

"Indigenous people?" Lunar asked, recognizing the deliberate modification.

Poppy nodded. "This was a ceremonial site, and possibly a refuge during conflicts. The lower chambers have water sources and multiple exits."

She secured her light and began descending with practiced skill, her movements sure despite the minimal illumination. Lunar could have simply flowed down as shadow essence, but maintained his semi-solid form to remain near her, ready to assist if needed.

When they reached the bottom, the air changed noticeably, becoming cooler and moister. The sound of running water reached them, a soft background murmur that would help mask their own sounds from pursuers.

"This way," Poppy directed, leading him along a narrow ledge beside an underground stream. The water reflected her red light in rippling patterns, creating complex shadow displays that Lunar found aesthetically pleasing.

Above them, faint vibrations indicated continued movement in the upper chambers. Lunar expanded his senses, monitoring the search patterns. The pursuers were thorough but cautious, suggesting they understood the potential dangers of the cave system.

After several minutes of careful progress, they reached a larger chamber where the stream widened into a small pool before disappearing into a rock wall. Poppy directed her light upward, revealing a ceiling studded with stone formations that hung like frozen raindrops.

"We should rest here briefly," she said, keeping her voice low. "The water masks sound."

Lunar extended his shadow awareness throughout the chamber, confirming her assessment. "Your knowledge of defensive positioning is impressive."

"When you work with animals that humans have pushed to the edge of extinction, you learn about hiding places," Poppy replied, settling onto a dry rock ledge.

"You protect endangered species," Lunar observed. "Even against your own kind."

"Some things are worth protecting, even when it's inconvenient for humans."

The statement resonated with Lunar in unexpected ways. Lunaris philosophy did not include the idea of protection rooted in inherent value rather than utility. The needs of the shadow territories had defined his entire existence.

"You never answered my question," Poppy said after a moment. "About what you're going to do. About your mission, about Earth, about us."

The directness of her question deserved equal directness in response. "My official report will be incomplete," Lunar stated. "Certain observations will be omitted."

"Meaning?"

"Meaning I will not recommend Earth for resource acquisition or strategic deployment," Lunar clarified. "Regardless of its objective value to the shadow territories."

Poppy studied him in the dim red light, her expression serious. "Because of me?"

"Partially," Lunar admitted. "But additionally, I have noticed aspects of Earth's existence that deserve preservation, like the balance between light and dark, the ability to adapt to change, and the freedom of self-determination."

"Things your world doesn't have," Poppy concluded.

"Things the shadow territories specifically lack."

"What does that mean for you personally?" Poppy pressed. "When Galaxy Brides comes back, will you leave with them?"

The question required Lunar to confront contradictions in his operational parameters. His loyalty to the shadow territories was absolute, ingrained through generations of genetic and cultural programming. However, his experience with Poppy introduced new factors that could not be easily reconciled with a simple return to his previous role.

"I do not know," he answered truthfully. "The optimal course of action remains unclear."

Poppy studied him for a long moment. He wished he could read inside her thoughts. Finally, she said, "Well, I guess first we need to survive Milano's hunting party. Then we can worry about interstellar travel plans."

A faint vibration traveled through the rock above them, followed by the distant sound of mechanical equipment. The search was expanding.

"Do you feel that?" She touched the rocky ground. "We should get moving."

She led him to the edge of the underground pool, where the water disappeared into the rock wall. "This is where it gets tricky. There's a submerged passage here that leads to another chamber. It's not long, maybe fifteen meters, but you have to swim through completely underwater."

Poppy dug inside her pack, pulled out a plastic container, and put her cell phone inside.

Lunar assessed the challenge. His shadow form could navigate the passage without difficulty, flowing through the smallest openings regardless of water content. But Poppy would face significant risk.

"No. This creates unacceptable danger for you," he stated.

"I've done it before," Poppy assured him. "I mapped this system last year. The passage is wide enough, and I know exactly where the air pocket is on the other side."

Despite her confident tone, he detected a shift in her energy. She was scared.

"The presence of Milano creates additional variables that you did not face when you mapped the cave. If they detect us, you could be trapped.

"Got a better idea?" Poppy challenged. "Because this is the only way to an exit that comes out in a completely different area."

Lunar considered alternatives. "There is another option. I can transport you through the passage."

"Transport me? How?"

"By extending my shadow field to encompass you," Lunar explained. "It would allow you to move as I do, through spaces that would normally be impassable."

Poppy's eyes widened. "You can do that? Turn me into a shadow?"

"Temporarily," Lunar clarified. "It is not without risk. No human has experienced the shadow state before. The effect on your biological systems is unknown."

Poppy considered this for only a moment before

nodding. "Let's do it. Better than drowning if something goes wrong in the underwater passage."

"The process requires complete physical contact," Lunar informed her. "My energy field must fully envelop yours."

Without hesitation, Poppy stepped closer, placing herself directly before him. "I trust you, Lunar."

He extended his arms, drawing Poppy against his shadow form. His energy field expanded, flowing around and through her physical body like water surrounding a stone. He felt her initial tension, then conscious relaxation as she surrendered to the process.

"Your heartrate has accelerated," he noted, monitoring her biological responses carefully.

"It feels incredible," Poppy whispered, her voice taking on an echoing quality as the shadow energy enveloped her more completely. "Cold but not unpleasant. Like being underwater but still able to breathe."

Lunar completed the energy transfer, fully incorporating Poppy into his shadow field. To an observer, they would appear as a single shadow entity, her physical form indistinguishable within his dark essence. He could feel every aspect of her biology now, the flow of blood through her veins, the electrical impulses of her nervous system, the exchange of oxygen in her lungs.

"Can you still hear me?" he asked, concerned about maintaining her consciousness during the transition.

"Yes," her voice responded from within his field. "It's like we're the same being. I can feel you everywhere."

"We must proceed quickly," Lunar advised. "Maintaining this state will drain your biological energy over time."

He moved them toward the underwater passage, flowing like liquid shadow across the surface of the pool. When they reached the submerged opening, Lunar simply continued forward, his shadow essence passing through the water as easily as it moved through air.

The passage twisted through solid rock, occasionally narrowing to spaces barely large enough for a human body to pass. Within Lunar's shadow field, such constraints meant nothing. They moved as a single fluid entity, navigating turns and constrictions that would have been impossible for Poppy in her physical form.

Lunar monitored her biological functions continuously, noting increased stress markers but nothing approaching dangerous levels. Her consciousness remained stable, her mental patterns indicating wonder beneath her fear.

They emerged into a larger chamber beyond the underwater passage, where Lunar gradually withdrew his shadow field, returning Poppy to her normal physical state. She stood unsteadily for a moment, her expression dazed as she readjusted to independent existence.

"That was," she began, then shook her head, apparently unable to find adequate words.

"Disorienting," Lunar supplied. "The transition between energy states often creates temporary sensory confusion."

"Amazing!" Poppy corrected. "I could feel everything you felt. The world looks completely different through the shadows."

Lunar had not anticipated this level of sharing. Typically, transported entities stayed aware of their own identity but did not have direct shadow perception. Poppy's experience suggested an unusually deep integration.

"Your adaptation was exceptional," he acknowledged. "Most beings resist shadow integration, creating friction that limits perceptual transfer."

"I told you, I've always been drawn to the dark," Poppy replied with a small smile. "You know, I have to ask. Did you learn our language from kidnapped astronauts or something? The way you say things is very scientifically precise."

"No. I have an implanted translator that makes my words understandable to you. I am saying things how we say them on my planet, and they come out in a way you can understand."

"Just curious." The corner of her mouth twitched at the side.

The chamber they had entered was larger than the previous one, with a ceiling high enough that Lunar could not detect its upper boundaries. A faint current of air suggested a connection to the surface, and the ambient temperature was slightly warmer.

"Where are we now?" Lunar asked, allowing Poppy to orient them in the unfamiliar space.

"Secondary cave system below the canyon," she explained, activating her red light again. "There's a concealed exit about half a kilometer from here that comes out near an unmarked trail. From there, we can reach the back roads and eventually a route, which connects to the main highway."

"They might have established surveillance on major transportation routes," Lunar noted.

"Probably," Poppy agreed. "But I know people at the wildlife sanctuary who can help us get transport without question."

"We should contact Eclipse and Solar," Lunar said. "Let them know where to find us."

"We will once I can get a phone signal," Poppy agreed. "There's a ridge near the exit where I can usually get cell reception."

They navigated the new cave system, with Poppy in the lead. The passages showed no signs of human visitation. There were no footpaths, just the raw, ancient stone shaped by water over millions of years.

After navigating several tight passages and climbing a natural stone chimney, they reached a narrow fissure that admitted a thin strip of late afternoon light.

"It looks like it's not yet evening," she noted. "Not ideal for you to be above ground, but we can find shadow cover in the canyon."

Lunar assessed the risk factors. Daylight would restrict his shadow-walking capabilities and increase his visibility to tracking technology. However, the benefits of contacting Eclipse and Solar outweighed these disadvantages, particularly given Milano's demonstrated search capabilities.

"I will manage," he assured her.

Poppy squeezed through the fissure first, checking for any sign of human presence before signaling Lunar to follow. The exit emerged behind a large boulder. Beyond, there was a steep-sided canyon whose walls cast considerable shadow.

"The ridge is this way," Poppy indicated, leading him along a nearly invisible game trail that climbed the canyon wall. "Stay close to the cliff face. The shadows are deeper there."

Lunar followed her guidance, keeping within the darkness cast by the towering red rocks. Poppy matched his careful progress.

When they reached the ridge, Poppy crouched behind a large juniper and checked her communication device. "Two bars. Not great, but it should work. Who do we call first?

"Eclipse," Lunar decided. "He will coordinate with Solar."

Poppy nodded and initiated the call. After several seconds, she shook her head. "Dammit. It's not going through."

From their elevated position, Lunar could see the expanse of the canyon below. In the distance, a familiar energy caught his attention.

"There," he pointed. "Energy discharges consistent with Solar's signature. He's there."

Poppy pulled out binoculars and adjusted her position to see better. "That's the retreat."

"Perhaps I should go to him," Lunar stated. "You should find somewhere safe to hide until this is over."

"Until what is over? Your Earth visit?" Poppy frowned and shook her head. "I'm not leaving you. We should move to lower ground before sunset. There's a hidden ravine about half a mile from here where we can wait for full darkness. The reception might be better there."

Lunar nodded.

He followed her for several minutes in silence. His mind calculated approach routes and tactical options. If Milano had deployed specialized counter-measures for Zorveyan energy signatures, direct confrontation would be ineffective. They needed an alternative strategy.

If anything happened to her, he would not survive it.

Suddenly, she stopped and leaned over. "We're going to need to find water before—"

A ringing noise interrupted her, and she straightened in surprise. Poppy grabbed her communication device and looked at it.

"It's Dani."

"Solar's fire tamer?"

Instead of answering him, she answered the call. "Dani? Is that you? Can you hear me?"

She paused speaking and frowned.

"We've got trouble. Some guys in Milano Enterprise SUVs found my place this morning. They've been hunting us. We're hiding in the canyon caves." Another pause. "Yes, he's with me. We're both fine."

She listened for a moment longer.

"We're about a mile past the big ridge," she said before relaying a condensed version of what happened to them.

She looked around before coming closer to him.

"Hold on. I'll put you on speaker." Poppy pushed a button. "Lunar is with me."

Lunar eyed the primitive communication tool.

"Eclipse and Solar?" Lunar asked.

"Safe. Here," Dani said. "Galaxy Brides has made contact with Solar. They're going to send coordinates where you can meet them."

"Extraction?" Lunar asked.

"Yes. In forty-eight hours," Dani confirmed.

"So soon?" Poppy stared at him, but he didn't know what she was trying to tell him with the look.

"Inform Eclipse that this Milano group has advanced tracking technology," Lunar said. "Their search protocols suggest military training and specialized equipment for detecting non-Earth energy signatures."

"That's what we were thinking," Dani agreed. "James Petersen, a Milano representative, approached Rowan and Eclipse last night. He referenced satellite data and electromagnetic anomalies from your arrival. Can you return to the retreat safely?"

Lunar glanced at Poppy, who was scanning the canyon.

"After nightfall," Poppy said.

"I'll tell them to expect you after dark," Dani said. "Be careful out there."

"You too." Poppy ended the call.

"I do not like this," Lunar stated. "I question Galaxy Alien Mail Order Brides' reliability given previous performance. We should act as if we will be on our own. Let's find a better location. We should assume Milano will continue their pursuit."

8

LUNAR MOVED THROUGH THE DESERT LIKE A living shadow, Poppy close behind him as they descended into a hidden ravine. It provided excellent cover. It was a natural trench that ran for nearly a mile through the red rock landscape.

"The ravine should keep us hidden until full dark," Poppy whispered as they reached the bottom of the steep slope. "Then I can approach the retreat from the western side to try to make contact with your friends. I'll bring them to where you're hiding if I can."

"Absolutely not." Lunar extended his shadow senses. "I will not send you into danger."

"We need to hurry," Poppy urged, her face tight

with concern. "They might need our help. We need a plan. I still think I should go alone."

"No," Lunar denied. "It is better if we stay together. I'm not sure they will remain at the retreat if it is unsafe. I will track their energy signatures."

Lunar had better tracking abilities than Solar and Eclipse combined. He had to be in tune with his terrain when living in darkness.

They traveled swiftly, stepping carefully over loose rocks and around patches of desert vegetation. Lunar's shadow form flowed effortlessly over the obstacles, while Poppy maintained an impressive pace for a human.

A sudden vibration in the earth made Lunar freeze. He extended a tendril of shadow essence upward, sensing the approach of vehicles along the ridge.

"Down," he commanded, pulling Poppy into a depression beneath an overhanging ledge.

They pressed against the cool rock as powerful beams of light swept the ravine from above. The harsh white illumination razored through the shadows, searching methodically for any sign of movement.

Lunar drew Poppy closer, extending his shadow

essence to envelop them both partially. Not enough for full shadow integration as he'd done in the underwater cave passage, but sufficient to blur their outlines against the natural shadows.

"Energy scanner," he whispered, feeling the distinctive pulse of Milano's detection technology.

Poppy's heartbeat accelerated against his chest, but her breathing remained controlled. His senses became distracted as he focused on her. His energy tried to flow into her like it had when they came together under the bioluminescence of their first cave. He very much wanted to transfer energy into her again.

A bright light drew his attention back into focus like a painful shock. The lights passed over their position once, then returned for a more focused sweep. Lunar condensed his shadow essence to its most compact form, suppressing his energy signature to the absolute minimum. The effort created a cold pressure in his core, like compressing a star into a black hole.

For an excruciating thirty seconds, the light remained fixed near their hiding place. Then, mercifully, it moved on, continuing its systematic search pattern along the ravine.

"We should keep moving," Lunar said as the vehicles receded. "They could come back around."

"How is any of this even possible?" Poppy asked. "I had the impression your kind hadn't been here before, but they're hunting like they know you. Or do all aliens have a signature? How many kinds of aliens are there?"

He heard a thread of panic building in her tone and didn't like it.

"Milano appears to possess advanced knowledge of extraterrestrial biology. This significantly increases the threat level," Lunar confirmed. "No, not all aliens are the same, and there are too many to count, so I cannot give you a number.

They resumed their journey through the ravine with increased caution. Lunar extended his senses to detect pursuit. The shadows deepened around them, bringing with them a renewal of his strength.

A distant explosion shattered the quiet, its concussive force traveling through the stone beneath their feet. Lunar extended his senses toward the source, analyzing the energy patterns.

"Solar and Eclipse are engaging defensive measures."

From their position, they witnessed flashes of

light coming from the retreat. Solar's energy signature was unmistakable. The golden flares of his defensive measures against Milano's forces illuminated the sky in brief, violent bursts until they culminated in an explosion. Now chaos emerged around the area.

"We need to hurry," Poppy urged, increasing her pace despite the treacherous footing.

The ravine began to curve toward the west, bringing them closer to the retreat. Lunar could sense a cluster of human energy signatures.

"Wait," he cautioned as they approached the end of the ravine. "Milano has deployed approximately twenty operatives on the ground with specialized equipment."

Poppy crouched beside him at the edge of their cover. "Can you see the Desert Suite from here?"

Lunar extended his shadow senses toward the retreat. The familiar structures emerged in his perception as patterns of thermal variances and electromagnetic signatures. The Desert Suite glowed with residual energy, a testament to recent conflict.

"Eclipse and Solar were there," he reported. "But their energy trails are moving underground."

"The lava tubes," Poppy realized. "There's an

entrance behind the meditation garden. They must be trying to escape through the underground network."

A new explosion illuminated the sky, followed by the distinctive hum of energy weapons. That was not primitive Earth technology. The sound signature matched Zorveyan defensive systems.

"We need to intercept them," Lunar decided, calculating the optimal approach route. "They're being pursued into the caves."

"I know those tunnels. There's a secondary entrance about a quarter mile from here. We can cut through and meet them inside."

Lunar assessed the tactical advantage of her suggestion. "Yes. Lead me."

Evening was finally claiming the land as they abandoned the ravine, crossing exposed terrain with rapid, careful movements. Lunar flowed between shadow patches, materializing only when necessary to ensure Poppy remained on course.

After several tense minutes, they reached a rocky outcropping with a narrow opening at its base. Poppy dropped to her hands and knees without hesitation, crawling into the dark aperture. Lunar followed, his shadow form easily navigating the restricted space. Her heavy breathing echoed around them.

"This tunnel is of volcanic origin. Ancient lava flows created a network of tubes beneath the surface," Poppy said, running her hand over the smooth walls that bore the swirling patterns of molten rock. She lifted her red light just enough to illuminate the path, allowing her to navigate safely. "This way. These tubes connect to the larger cave system."

They moved swiftly through the underground passage, the sounds of conflict growing louder ahead. Shouts echoed through the stone corridors, punctuated by the distinctive discharge of energy weapons.

A powerful vibration shook loose stones from the ceiling. Dust filled the air.

"They're using explosives," Poppy coughed, covering her mouth. "They can't do that. These caves are precious."

Lunar frowned as he detected a pressure wave. "That's not Milano. It feels like Eclipse. He wouldn't do that unless they were trying to escape."

Poppy increased her pace, navigating the twisting passage. "There's a junction ahead where multiple tunnels converge. If we can reach it first—"

Another explosion, closer this time, sent a shock wave through the tunnel system. Poppy fell back against the wall. Larger rocks began to fall around them.

"Structural integrity compromised," Lunar warned, extending his shadow field to deflect falling debris away from Poppy.

He swept her forward until they reached a larger chamber where three tunnels converged into a natural cavern. The space bore evidence of recent conflict, including scorch marks on the walls, scattered equipment, and the lingering resonance of Solar's energy discharges.

"They were here," Poppy confirmed, examining fresh footprints in the dust. "Not long ago."

Lunar extended his senses, searching for familiar energy signatures. "Solar's pattern is detectable. Moving away from us, deeper into the system." He paused, focusing on a fainter trace. "Eclipse's signature is weaker. Possibly injured."

"Which tunnel?" Poppy asked urgently.

Before Lunar could respond, a new sound reached them. It was the methodical approach of multiple pursuers. Flashlight beams played across the walls of the tunnel they had just emerged from.

"Milano forces," Lunar warned, pulling Poppy toward the far side of the chamber where shadows were deepest.

They pressed against the wall as four black-clad operatives entered the cavern, their equipment emitting the distinctive hum of energy scanners. Each carried weapons, but unlike standard Earth firearms, they were more compact with a bluish glow emanating from their power cores.

"Energy signatures detected in section B-7," one reported into a communication device. "Proceeding with containment protocol. Don't let this one get away."

Lunar analyzed their equipment with growing concern. The weapons appeared to be modified versions of Zorveyan technology, specifically designed to counter shadow manipulation.

His essence condensed into its most defensive configuration as he kept Poppy trapped behind him. He felt her trembling.

The operatives searched the chamber, their scanners sweeping across the walls and floor. When one of the beams passed near their position, it emitted a higher-pitched tone.

"Contact," the operative announced sharply. "Northwest quadrant."

All four turned in their direction, weapons raised. Lunar made an instant tactical decision.

"When I move, run to the right tunnel," he

instructed Poppy through their connection so the others couldn't hear. *"Find Solar and Eclipse. I will divert them."*

Before she could protest, Lunar expanded his shadow essence explosively outward, plunging the entire chamber into absolute darkness by absorbing all available light. The Milano operatives shouted in confusion as their flashlights and scanners suddenly became useless.

Poppy did not hesitate. She slipped away in the direction Lunar had indicated, her footsteps nearly silent on the stone floor.

Lunar projected multiple shadow decoys throughout the chamber, each emitting a partial energy signature to confuse the scanners. The Milano operatives fired blindly, their weapons releasing pulses of disruptive energy that stung when they passed through his dispersed form.

One operative activated a different device, and suddenly, harsh white light flooded the chamber, powerful enough to penetrate even Lunar's shadow manipulation. The tactical disadvantage was immediate and severe. His shadow form recoiled from the intense illumination, forced to consolidate.

"Target acquired," the operative announced. "Deploying energy containment field."

Lunar did not wait to be trapped. He flowed across the chamber like liquid darkness, engulfing the light source and the operative who held it. The human shouted in alarm as cold shadow essence enveloped him. He dropped the device as he grabbed for his neck, choking for air. Lunar did not kill him. When the device dropped, he crushed it, plunging the chamber back into darkness.

The remaining operatives fired in the direction of the disturbance. The human who dropped the light was struck by several of the stray blasts. He screamed in pain.

Their energy pulses disrupted portions of Lunar's shadow field. The sensation was painful but manageable. He reacted by generating a whirl of shadow energy to confuse their sensors.

With the operatives temporarily disoriented, Lunar flowed toward the tunnel Poppy had taken. He detected her energy signature moving swiftly ahead, already beyond immediate danger. Relief filled him.

As Lunar retreated into the tunnel, the operatives regrouped, activating secondary light sources and preparing to pursue. He needed to delay them further to ensure Poppy's escape.

Reaching out with tendrils of shadow essence,

Lunar located structural weaknesses in the tunnel ceiling. He pressed hard to trigger a controlled collapse behind him. Rocks tumbled down, blocking the passage without causing catastrophic failure of the entire system. Poppy would not like it, but he did it to protect her.

9

ON THE RUN WITH AN ALIEN.

This was insane.

Half the time, she thought she was trapped in a nightmare, but then Lunar would touch her. His energy grounded her. He was the most real thing she'd ever experienced in her life.

Poppy's heart raced as she followed Lunar through the winding tunnel. The cave system had been her sanctuary for years, a place where she'd mapped and explored the hidden world beneath Duskrock's red rocks. Never had she imagined using that knowledge to escape alien hunters. Or that she would see the precious landscape caved in during it.

Ahead of them, the passage forked into three separate tunnels. Lunar paused, his shadow form rippling as he searched the area. Despite everything, she felt safe with him and his abilities.

"Milano forces have dug through the rocks and are approaching from behind," he said, his voice carrying the calm she'd come to find oddly comforting. "And I detect Solar's energy signature ahead. He's weakened and moving slowly with a human companion."

"That must be Rowan or Dani," Poppy said. "Which tunnel?"

Lunar indicated the central passage. "There. But the Milano operatives will be upon us within minutes."

She studied the three tunnels, her mind racing through the mental map she'd built over years of exploration. "The left tunnel circles back toward the entrance. The middle one leads deeper, eventually connecting to a vertical shaft that exits near my friend Mack's property. The right one leads to a narrower passage system that only someone who knows the caves can navigate."

Lunar turned to her, his darkness somehow more solid, more present than it had been before. "We must separate."

"What? No." The words escaped before she could stop them, her chest tightening at the thought.

"It is tactically necessary," Lunar insisted. "I must intercept Solar and assist his escape. He will not be doing well in this darkness. You must reach the surface and secure transportation."

She wanted to argue, but the rational part of her brain knew he was right. "Mack has a cabin deeper in the wilderness. He said something about using some kind of special roofing material that blocks helicopter scans, or something, I was only half listening, if I'm honest. He also has vehicles hidden around the canyon that can handle this terrain. He's a bit of an end-of-the-world conspiracy theorist. He told me how to find them in case I needed to escape when the new world regime releases a zombie-causing plague. I can secure transportation for us."

"This Mack is trustworthy?"

"Eccentric, but yes. Completely trustworthy. He's been helping me rescue animals for years. Doesn't ask questions."

Lunar seemed to consider this. "A cabin would provide temporary shelter while we reassess our options."

Another distant boom shook the cave, sending dust drifting down from the ceiling. Milano was getting closer.

"We need to hurry," Poppy said. "The middle

passage will take you to Solar. I'll take the right one to a different exit, get a vehicle, and meet you at the northern shaft exit. To find it, you—"

"Directions are not necessary. I will find you." Lunar moved closer, his body coalescing into his more humanoid form. "This plan carries significant risk. Milano's forces are well-equipped and organized."

"I know these caves better than anyone except maybe Mack," she assured him. "I'll be fine."

For a moment, Lunar was silent, his star-like patterns swirling more rapidly within his darkness. Then, unexpectedly, he reached out and touched her face with what felt like cool mist given form.

"Your shadow compatibility is..." He paused, as if searching for words. "Unique. Valuable."

Poppy smiled, recognizing the sentiment behind his clinical description. "Are you saying you'll miss me?"

"The concept of missing implies an emotional attachment that shadow operatives are not supposed to cultivate." His voice dropped lower. "Yet I find myself experiencing precisely such an attachment."

The admission sent warmth spreading through her chest. Without hesitation, she stepped forward, closing the distance between them. "I'll miss you too."

For a moment, they stood there, her warmth meeting his coolness, creating that strange harmony that resonated between them. Then, acting on instinct, she leaned in and pressed her lips to where his would be if he were human.

Electricity flowed between them, his essence partially enveloping her, creating a circuit of energy that made her skin tingle and her breath catch. Lunar's star-light patterns pulsed an accelerated rhythm like a quickened heartbeat.

"Although I appreciate the human sex offer, we do not have the time for proper energy transferring."

"It's just something to remember me by," she said with a small smile. "Be safe."

"I do not require reminders. You have altered my energy patterns in ways that cannot be forgotten." His hand brushed her cheek again. "Be cautious, Poppy Jensen."

Another explosion, closer now, shook the tunnel.

"Go," she urged. "Find them. I'll meet you at the northern exit with transportation as soon as I can."

Lunar hesitated only a moment longer, the swirling patterns within his darkness conveying emotions his words did not. Then he flowed away, his shadow form disappearing into the central tunnel.

Poppy watched until the last tendril of darkness

vanished, then turned toward her own escape route. The right tunnel narrowed quickly, requiring her to crouch as she navigated its twisting path. Her red-filtered flashlight cast just enough illumination to avoid obstacles without betraying her position.

Behind her, she heard the sounds of boots on stone, the electronic hum of scanning equipment, and voices calling out coordinates to one another. Milano's forces were methodical and well-equipped, but they didn't have her knowledge of the cave system's secret paths.

The passage narrowed further until she had to turn sideways to squeeze through a fissure barely visible unless you knew exactly where to look. Beyond it, the tunnel dropped sharply before opening into a lower level of caves that tourists never saw.

As she descended, Poppy felt the connection to Lunar stretching but not breaking. Since their first encounter outside The Crash Zone, she'd been able to sense his presence, his unique energy signature that resonated with something deep within her. Now, even separated by stone and distance, she could feel the faint pull of his shadow essence, like a compass pointing toward true north.

The sensation both comforted and worried her. If

she could sense him, could Milano's technology do the same? If he left Earth, would she lose this connection? Or would it carry on through the stars like a heartache that would haunt her for the rest of her life?

The lower passage wound through a series of small chambers, some bearing ancient pictographs left by indigenous peoples. Poppy moved efficiently, her years of mapping these tunnels allowing her to navigate even the most confusing intersections without hesitation.

After twenty minutes of careful progress, she reached a narrow chimney that led upward toward the surface. Natural handholds worn into the rock face made climbing possible, though still challenging in the dim red light. She secured her flashlight between her teeth and began to ascend, careful to test each handhold before trusting it with her weight.

The vertical shaft rose nearly thirty feet before opening onto the desert surface. Poppy emerged behind a large boulder, perfectly concealed from casual observation. Mack had a vehicle parked nearby. She started to go for it, but then stopped. It wouldn't make sense to take it out of hiding until they were ready to leave. The afternoon sun still hung in the sky, forcing her to shield her eyes after so long in the cave darkness. She found shelter in the shadow of a large rock formation and waited, her senses attuned to any sign of Lunar's shadow energy.

Minutes stretched and filled her with worry. The sun began its descent toward the horizon, painting the red rocks in deeper shades of crimson. Still no sign of Lunar or the others. Worry gnawed at her stomach. Had Milano captured them? Had the tunnels collapsed?

Just as she was considering the risky move of returning to the caves to search for them, she felt a flicker of cold energy, like a shadow passing over her consciousness. Lunar was approaching, but something felt different. His energy signature was altered, carrying another frequency within it.

Poppy moved closer to the cave entrance, staying within the shadow of the rocks. A flicker of darkness emerged from the opening, flowing like liquid night before solidifying into Lunar's more defined form.

"Lunar," she instantly wrapped her arms around him. "Thank goodness you're okay. Did you find them?"

He held her against him, as if absorbing the feel of her into his body. "I found Solar's fire-tamer, Dani. She is injured. I believe she needs medical attention. If it is safe, take her and come back."

"Where is she?"

Lunar gestured at the opening. "I have to leave you again."

"But—" He disappeared into a crevice before she could answer.

Poppy went in and found Dani leaning against a cave wall, breathing heavily.

"Dani," Poppy exclaimed, relief flooding through her. "Thank goodness. Lunar said you need a doctor?"

"No. I just twisted my ankle," Dani waved a hand in dismissal as if it didn't matter, but she winced as she shifted her weight. "I'm more worried about Solar. Have you seen him?"

Poppy shook her head in denial. "Not since the retreat. Lunar's been tracking energy signatures through the caves, but Milano's equipment is interfering."

Poppy reached down to give Dani a hand as she squeezed through the narrow opening, supporting her as they emerged onto the sun-baked ledge high on the canyon wall. Dani limped badly as she found her footing.

"Here, give me that." Poppy grabbed the backpack Dani was carrying to help.

"That's their tech," Dani said.

"What tech?" Poppy asked, steadying Dani as she stumbled.

"Rowan called Pete from the crystal shop to cause a distraction. Marvin, one of his alien enthusiast friends, managed to grab some items from the suite before Milano took over. Devices, something Lunar called an energy stone... I don't know what they do, but I figured they shouldn't fall into Milano's hands."

"Good thinking. Even seemingly innocuous alien tech could be dangerous if reverse-engineered." Poppy glanced to where Lunar had disappeared. She wanted to go in after him. Instead, she carried the bag. Dani was in no shape to be left alone in the desert. "There's a jeep hidden about a quarter mile from here. We need to get moving. Milano's got helicopters searching the area."

To prove her point, the threat of a helicopter echoed over them.

Seriously, fuck these Milano thugs. Why couldn't they just let the aliens be?

Poppy guided Dani along the narrow ledge, her hand steady despite her racing heart. Five years of rescuing injured animals from these canyons had taught her how to move efficiently while supporting deadweight. Dani was far from deadweight, though. The fire dancer had a stubborn determination that reminded Poppy of the desert predators she rehabilitated. Wounded but refusing to yield.

Tourists were ever changing, but the local residents tended to stick together. Poppy knew Dani, but not to the point where they hung out or made plans together. Still, she felt a kinship with the woman. They were both in the same boat. They were in love with extraterrestrials.

Love. It was hard for her to admit that.

Still, that's what she felt. Love.

The path widened ahead, a small mercy that allowed them to pick up pace. Poppy's ears caught the distinctive rhythm of helicopter blades before her eyes spotted the black shape cresting the ridge.

"Down," she ordered, yanking Dani behind a rust-colored boulder that had stood sentinel since before humans wrecked the Earth.

The stone radiated stored heat against her back as they pressed themselves flat. Poppy felt the shadow of the helicopter slide across them like an icy finger, leaving her skin prickling with awareness. Milano's hunters. So close. So determined. Such assholes.

Her thoughts turned to Lunar, still in those caves. Would his shadow abilities protect him from Milano's specialized equipment? The moments they'd shared had created something much more profound than a physical connection. The resonance hummed between them even now, across distance and stone. If Milano captured him...

She couldn't bear the thought.

The helicopter passed, its sound fading as it continued its search pattern. Poppy exhaled, then guided Dani forward through a labyrinth of rock formations she knew by heart. Each turn brought them closer to safety and further from Lunar. The contradiction twisted in her chest.

The jeep had been hidden in a dry wash, beneath a natural overhang where old flash floods had carved out a hollow in the sandstone. Mack had positioned it perfectly, as always. The old geologist understood the desert's secrets better than anyone except perhaps Poppy herself.

"Nice ride," Dani commented, eyeing the battered vehicle.

"It knows these canyons better than any Milano SUV," Poppy replied, unable to suppress a flash of pride. The Wrangler had saved more animals—*and now, apparently, aliens*—than any fancy corporate vehicle ever could. She helped Dani into the passenger seat, then examined her ankle. The swelling suggested a serious sprain, possibly torn ligaments. "This needs ice."

She reached for the first aid kit Mack always kept under the seat, only to find it missing. "Dammit. I forgot to restock."

After their last rescue of a juvenile bobcat with a paw caught in an illegal trap, she'd used all the supplies and meant to replace them. One more thing gone wrong today.

"It'll be okay," Dani said, rubbing her calf as if to soothe the pain in her ankle. "What's the plan?"

Poppy's mind raced through options, mapping routes and safe houses like the cave systems she'd spent years documenting. "I know a place about twenty miles into the backcountry. Off-grid cabin, no electricity, no cell service. Milano won't find us there." She glanced instinctively toward the cave entrance they'd emerged from, feeling that strange pull toward Lunar again. "I told Lunar we'd go there once he finds the others."

"If he finds them," Dani voiced what Poppy couldn't bring herself to say.

Poppy reached out, giving Dani's shoulder a gentle squeeze. The woman's skin radiated unusual heat. A vestige of her connection to Solar, perhaps? "He'll find them. Lunar may seem cold, but he's incredibly determined." She thought of his shadow essence, how it flowed with such purpose and never wasted motion. "And Solar strikes me as the type who'd burn through a mountain to get back to someone he cares about."

They both stared toward the cave as if in a silent debate about what to do. Poppy didn't want to think about what would happen if the others didn't make it out of the caves. She couldn't face that possibility.

Poppy listened to the sky, anticipating when she should drive.

"We need supplies," Dani said. "Food, water, first aid. If they're injured when they get out..."

Poppy's mind clicked into rescue mode. "Can you ride?"

"Ride?" Dani raised an eyebrow.

"Crotch-rocket."

"Yeah, but..." Dani glanced around, her confusion evident.

"Good. I'm taking you to the animal clinic. I'll drop you off and come back here to get the others." The plan took shape as she spoke. "You wrap that ankle, stock up on first aid and supplies, then meet back up with us. The staff motorcycle is around the back of the building. Take it."

The helicopter's thrum returned, growing louder.

Poppy ducked down, pulling Dani with her until they were practically lying across the seats. The black shape passed overhead, its searchlight sweeping the terrain dangerously close to their position.

When it passed, Poppy's fingers found the ignition. The jeep rumbled to life, the sound comforting in its familiar imperfection. "Hold tight," she warned. "This isn't going to be a smooth ride."

She navigated by instinct more than sight, following invisible trails only recognizable to those who read the desert's subtle language. The jeep bounced and jolted, each impact sending shock waves through the frame. Poppy winced sympathetically at Dani's poorly concealed pain, but maintained their pace. Speed was safety now.

From the corner of her eye, she noticed Dani constantly looking back toward the cave system, searching the horizon. The dancer's connection to Solar was as palpable as Poppy's to Lunar. Two humans inexplicably bound to alien beings they'd known for mere days.

"We'll find them," Poppy said softly, recognizing the fear in Dani's eyes.

The words were as much for herself as for Dani. Lunar would return. He had to. That cool electricity they'd shared, that perfect resonance between his shadow and her light. It couldn't end now, not when she'd finally found someone who understood the darkness she'd always carried within.

Dani nodded silently, turning her attention forward. The sun continued its descent, painting the landscape in deepening reds and purples. The lengthening shadows seemed alive with possibility, dark fingers reaching across the desert floor.

They drove in tense silence, each lost in her own thoughts. The animal clinic appeared ahead, its simple structure a promise of supplies and temporary safety for Dani.

Poppy pulled around back, already estimating how quickly she could return to the cave exit. Every minute away from Lunar felt like stretching a vital connection thinner, risking it might snap altogether. Poppy gave Dani directions on where to meet them.

"If anyone could find Solar and Eclipse in the darkness of those caves, it would be Lunar," Poppy assured her. She barely gave Dani time to get out before speeding away. The jeep's dust cloud hung in the air. Her heart ached at leaving the injured woman behind, but she knew Dani was resourceful, and more importantly, she needed to get back to Lunar and the others before Milano closed in.

The drive back to the cave exit felt agonizingly slow despite pushing the vibrating jeep to its limits. Twilight was settling over the desert by the time she approached the ridge where she hoped to find them waiting. She killed the engine a quarter-mile away and coasted to a stop behind a large boulder, not wanting the sound to draw unwanted attention.

From this vantage point, she had a clear view of the cave exit. The sun had dropped behind the western mountains, casting long shadows across the canyon. They were perfect conditions for Lunar's shadow abilities.

Poppy closed her eyes, focusing on their connection. She sensed his presence, a cool spot in her awareness that pulsed with quiet energy.

He was close.

He was safe.

Her eyes snapped open as she felt a surge in the shadow energy. Peering around the boulder, she saw movement at the cave entrance, a flicker of darkness that materialized into Lunar's more defined form. Behind him came Rowan, looking exhausted but determined, and finally Solar, his golden energy noticeably dimmed.

Poppy stepped forward into a shaft of fading light, making herself visible to them.

"Over here," she called softly.

Lunar's head turned instantly toward her voice, the star-like patterns within his darkness swirling faster. Without words, he guided Solar and Rowan toward her position, his movements protective.

"Hurry," she urged as they approached. "Helicopters are coming."

The hair on the back of Poppy's neck stood up a split second before her ears caught the sound of their return. The rhythmic thump of helicopter blades sliced through the evening air. Her body tensed on instinct, the way it did when she sensed a predator while working with injured wildlife.

"Where's Eclipse?" she asked.

"Still in the caves." Rowan looked like she might cry. "He stayed behind to fight off Milano."

Poppy frowned. "We need to go back for him. No one gets left behind."

"No time," Lunar denied.

A black helicopter emerged over the canyon ridge, its rotors cutting through the desert air. Beneath, dust clouds billowed upward from several vehicles traveling along the trails.

"They're preparing to flush us out," Lunar said.

· · ·

"THIS WAY," she directed, moving toward the hidden jeep. Every second counted now.

"That's your transportation?" Solar asked skeptically.

"It's better than walking," Poppy quipped. She didn't know what Dani saw in the alien. He was kind of an ass. "And it knows these trails better than any fancy SUV."

As she moved, she couldn't help but notice how Solar's normally radiant form had dimmed to a muted glow, like a campfire burning down to embers. His golden energy flickered and wavered with each step. The sight sent a shiver down her spine. If Milano could weaken a being of pure light that severely, what might they do to Lunar?

"What about Dani?" Rowan asked. "She was supposed to warn you about the attack."

Poppy slid behind the wheel as they all piled in, not bothering to answer yet. Her gaze narrowed in on the ignition, her fingers automatically finding the hidden switch Mack had installed below the steering column, a backup system for when the standard ignition failed, which happened more often than not with this ancient vehicle. The engine caught with a cough and rumble that vibrated through the frame.

"What about Dani?" Rowan asked, turning in her

seat. "She was supposed to warn you about the attack."

Poppy glanced in the rearview mirror, catching Solar leaning forward, his energy field pulsing like a heartbeat. The golden alien might pretend indifference, but his body betrayed him. He cared for the fire dancer, perhaps more than he understood himself.

"We found her in the caves looking for you," Poppy explained, throwing the jeep into gear and feeling the familiar resistance of the old transmission. "She escaped the retreat in an alien flash mob of all things. She's meeting us at the rendezvous point with supplies."

The relief that washed through Solar was almost palpable. His dimmed light brightened momentarily before he reined it in. Poppy caught Lunar's gaze in the rearview mirror, a silent understanding passing between them. They'd both recognized what the others might not yet admit. This wasn't just about survival anymore. Something deeper had formed between aliens and humans, connections that defied the boundaries of their worlds.

The jeep lurched over a rock, the suspension groaning in protest. Poppy focused her attention on the steering wheel to keep them from bouncing off course.

She'd driven these canyons in every condition—midnight rescues during monsoon season, blistering summer days when the metal of the vehicle would burn skin on contact, dawn trips to release rehabilitated animals back into their territories. But never with an alien shadow-being sitting behind her, his cool energy reaching out to brush against her consciousness like gentle fingers.

Even without looking back, she could feel Lunar's presence as a permanent link between them. The sensation was both comforting and distracting. She needed to focus on the treacherous terrain, but her awareness kept splitting between the physical world and that strange energetic connection.

The helicopter's spotlight swept across the terrain thirty yards to their left. Poppy jerked the wheel, guiding them deeper into the shadows of a rock formation. Her heart hammered against her ribs, but her hands remained steady.

Whatever happened next, Lunar had changed her forever. The shadow frequencies she'd always sensed, always been drawn to, now had meaning beyond her grandmother's vague explanations about "the sight." She'd found someone who existed within those frequencies, who understood that darkness wasn't emptiness but a presence with its own beauty. And she wouldn't give him up without a fight.

The helicopter veered away, continuing its search pattern in the wrong direction. Poppy allowed herself a small smile and pressed harder on the accelerator, steering them toward the deepest wilderness where Mack's cabin waited.

As they rounded a bend in the canyon, a lone figure appeared in the path ahead, illuminated by the jeep's headlights.

"There," Lunar said.

Poppy's heart leapt with recognition. Dani stood in the desert, waving her arms frantically, her posture betraying both pain and determination. The motorcycle she must have taken from the clinic was nowhere in sight.

Poppy felt Solar's energy surge behind her, his dimmed light suddenly brightening with an intensity that cast golden shadows across the dashboard. Without conscious thought, she was already turning the wheel, guiding the jeep toward the fire dancer.

Dani limped forward as they approached, her face tight with pain but her eyes alight with relief as they locked onto Solar's glowing form in the back seat. Poppy brought the vehicle to a stop beside her, dust billowing around them in a protective cloud.

Dani's voice was barely audible over the idling engine, and Poppy didn't hear what she said as she caught Lunar's gaze in the rearview mirror.

With Dani safely aboard, squeezed in beside Solar despite the cramped quarters, Poppy pressed the accelerator once more. The jeep surged forward, carrying its precious cargo deeper into the desert night where Mack's hidden cabin waited.

They were alive and mostly together, but they were still missing Eclipse. She had to believe Milano wouldn't kill him if they caught up to him. They'd want to take the aliens alive. And somehow, that felt like enough to hold onto as they fled into the gathering darkness.

10

Lunar sensed the approaching aircraft before the others heard it. The sound was different from Milano's helicopters. Higher-pitched. Irregular. Familiar in the worst possible way.

As they turned into the canyon, the whine grew louder.

"Incoming aerial vehicle," Solar warned unnecessarily.

Lunar frowned.

Galaxy Alien Mail Order Brides.

"What do I do?" Poppy yelled.

"Get off the trail," Solar ordered. "Find cover."

Poppy quickly complied, slowing down and guiding the jeep behind a cluster of large boulders.

"That flight pattern seems familiar," Lunar told Solar.

A flickering light appeared over the ridge, wobbling in a flight pattern that defied common sense. The Galaxy Brides transport pod came into view, its hull patched with what appeared to be... Lunar frowned. He seemed to remember humans called it duct tape.

Their odds of survival had just plummeted.

"No," Solar groaned beside him. "Not them."

Lunar agreed with the Solarian.

"Who?" Dani asked.

"Bob, Gary, and Pudding," Lunar answered.

"Bob and Gary," Solar replied simultaneously.

The pod lurched toward the ground, landing struts deploying unevenly. Dust billowed as the engines sputtered and died. The hatch opened, and Gary's yellow face peered out with inappropriate cheerfulness.

"Hello! Yoo-hoo! We've come to rescue you!"

"They're going to get us all killed," Solar muttered as Gary and Bob awkwardly climbed out of the craft.

Lunar studied their poorly fitted skin-suits with distaste. They looked like unattractive Earth children with oversized heads. Their arrival complicated an already desperate situation.

Gary jumped in excitement, as if this were a friendly meeting and they weren't on the run from Earth mercenaries. "There you are!"

Lunar leaned up to touch Poppy's shoulder. She shivered but put her hand over his.

"*You are safe,*" Lunar assured her, speaking so only she could hear him.

She gave a slight nod and squeezed his hand.

"We've been searching everywhere for you," Gary announced as he reached the jeep. "The extraction coordinates have been compromised. Milano has the entire area under surveillance." He stopped to count the occupants. "Oh dear. We weren't expecting so many of you."

"The extraction is still proceeding?" Solar asked.

"Of course," Bob interjected. "Just relocated. And accelerated. As in, right now. Our window is closing rapidly."

"Weren't there three of you?" Gary frowned, looking from Solar to Lunar.

"We can't find Eclipse," Rowan said, her voice tense with worry. "Can you track him?"

"Eclipse, that's right," Gary said vaguely.

"Ignore him. He bumped his foot." Bob slapped Gary's mouth.

Lunar glanced at the pod. It was too small and damaged. "Your pod cannot accommodate all of us."

"Well, no," Gary admitted, fidgeting. "It's really only designed for three passengers plus pilot. Four if everyone breathes in shifts."

"Then it's useless to us," Rowan said. "We're not leaving anyone behind."

"Actually," Bob insisted. "Milano's forces are converging on this location as we speak. They might have detected our landing."

"What?" Poppy demanded. "You led them straight to us?"

"Not intentionally," Gary protested. "But our stealth systems are, shall we say, somewhat compromised by the emergency repairs."

"How long until they reach us?" Solar asked.

"Twenty Earth minutes, perhaps less," Bob replied. "They're mobilizing from multiple directions."

Lunar quickly considered their options. Milano was closing in. Galaxy Alien Mail Order Brides offered a limited escape. The damaged pod would be tracked easily. Then again, they weren't exactly stealth driving on the ground either.

"We need to split up," Lunar stated. "Increase

survival probability through diversification of targets."

"Precisely what we were thinking," Gary exclaimed, too loudly. "Inverse targets."

"No," Rowan said immediately. "We stay together until we find Eclipse."

"The pod can transport the two of you to the new extraction coordinates," Bob said, sounding very much like he'd decided this as their leader. "The humans can continue by ground as decoys."

"Eclipse can take care of himself," Lunar stated, though he knew the twilight-dweller's chances weren't good against Milano's weapons.

"The cabin I was telling you about is still the safest immediate option," Poppy insisted. "We should all go there and regroup."

"The others can continue to the cabin location in the Earth vehicle, where we can arrange secondary extraction once the heat is off," Bob persisted.

Lunar exchanged a glance with Solar. For once, they agreed. Splitting up was their best chance.

"Solar and Dani should go with them," Lunar said, surprising everyone. "Solar's energy signature is the most detectable, especially now as we face darkness. He is the most likely to draw Milano to all of us.

And Dani requires medical attention that the extraction vessel can provide."

"What? No," Dani protested, turning to him with dismay. "My ankle is fine. We're not leaving you guys to face Milano alone."

"It's strategically sound," Solar said. "Milano developed specific countermeasures for our energy signatures. If Solar and I remain together, capture probability increases substantially."

A distant rumble interrupted them, followed by the thump of helicopter rotors.

"Decision time," Gary insisted nervously. "Milano's air support is incoming."

Solar decided for them. "Dani and I will go with you. Lunar, protect them." He nodded toward Rowan and Poppy. "We will search for Eclipse from the sky, and we will rendezvous at the secondary extraction point once it's secured."

"Wait," Dani began, but Solar had already moved, lifting her carefully from the jeep despite her protests. "We can't go into... We can't fly... I mean, up there?"

Solar carried her toward the pod. Dani's protests continued.

"You should drive now. Those helicopters will be

on us in minutes," Gary stated, already hurrying back toward the pod.

Lunar watched as Solar carried Dani into the pod, surprised by the Solarian's gentleness. The light-dweller's attachment to the human had grown. It was a transformation that Lunar recognized within himself.

These Earth women were changing them.

Lunar moved closer to Poppy, his shadow essence automatically adjusting to shield her. The cool darkness of his form met her warmth, creating that strange harmony he'd come to crave.

"Don't drive," he told her, extending his shadow field partly around her.

The pod's engines whined to life, wobbling dangerously before accelerating away with Solar and Dani aboard.

Almost immediately, the Milano helicopter changed course, its searchlight fixing on the departing pod. The diversion had worked. Solar's distinctive energy signature had drawn their pursuit.

"Now we move," Lunar directed. "Quickly, while their attention is diverted."

Lunar positioned himself to provide the vehicle with maximum shadow coverage. With Solar gone, it was much easier. Poppy started the engine and accelerated.

"Will they be okay?" Rowan asked, worry evident in her voice as she watched the sky.

"Solar's energy will regenerate quickly in space," Lunar responded. "And Galaxy Brides, despite their flaws, have transported many species."

"And Eclipse?" Rowan pressed.

Lunar hesitated. He preferred precision, not false hope. Yet the human's distress affected him strangely.

"Eclipse is resourceful," he stated finally. "His twilight abilities let him adapt to both light and shadow. His diplomatic training would serve him well if captured."

As they drove deeper into the wilderness, Lunar maintained his protective field around the vehicle, absorbing light to reduce their visibility. Poppy's proximity created that familiar resonance in his energy. The connection between them grew stronger despite circumstances.

"How much further to the cabin?" he asked.

"Not far," Poppy replied. "The worst of the terrain is behind us."

Lunar noticed the subtle changes when she spoke to him. Her quickened heartbeat, her slightly elevated temperature. He experienced similar reactions, the star-patterns within his darkness realigning whenever they interacted.

This connection between them represented both vulnerability and unexpected strength. It had changed his mission.

Changed him.

As they continued toward the hidden cabin, Lunar faced a choice he'd never anticipated. Return to the shadow territories with intelligence about Earth's defenses? Or remain with the human whose energy had become intertwined with his own?

For the first time in his existence, the path forward wasn't clear.

11

Lunar remained silent as they drove, scanning their surroundings for threats. Poppy guided the jeep down the final slope, branches scraping against the sides as they navigated the overgrown track.

"There," she said, pointing to a weathered structure that seemed to grow from the red rock itself. The cabin's log walls had aged to match the surrounding sandstone, camouflaged by decades of desert patina. "Mack built this forty years ago when he first started his geological surveys. No electricity, no running water, but it's got a well and a wood stove. No people around for at least three miles in any direction."

The cabin was exactly what they needed, a

forgotten relic, hidden so deep in the canyon that even seasoned locals would struggle to find it.

She watched Lunar extend his shadow senses, scanning for threats. "The isolation is advantageous."

"That's the idea," Poppy said, cutting the engine. The sudden silence was profound. There were no helicopters, no pursuit vehicles, just the whisper of wind through the juniper branches.

She took a deep breath, as if to steady herself before turning her attention to her friend.

Rowan climbed out first, her movements stiff with exhaustion. "How long can we stay here?"

"As long as we need to," Poppy replied, retrieving supplies from the back of the jeep. "Mack only comes up here during his quarterly surveys. We've got at least two months before he's due back. Even then, he won't care if we're here."

'They entered the cabin, dust motes dancing in the shaft of moonlight that slanted through a single window. The interior was sparse but functional with a wood stove in one corner, a rough table with two chairs, and a narrow cot against the far wall. The shelves lined with canned goods and water jugs reinforced that Mack had maintained plenty of emergency supplies.

"I'll get a fire going," Poppy said, moving toward the stove. "The nights get cold out here."

Lunar watched her work, noting how she navigated the dark cabin without hesitation. Her shadow compatibility continued to manifest in subtle ways.

Rowan walked with a hand sweeping through the darkness. Her leg bumped a cot and she sank onto it, cradling something against her chest. Lunar recognized the distinctive glow of Eclipse's energy stone that Dani had recovered from their suite at the retreat.

"He's still alive," Rowan whispered, her fingers tightening around the stone. "I know he is. I can feel him. Faint, but he's out there."

"Milano would keep him alive," Lunar confirmed. When he saw Rowan's expression, he tried to keep his doubts about Eclipse's condition to himself. "His diplomatic status and unique physiology make him valuable for study."

The word *study* made Rowan flinch, but she nodded, drawing strength from even this cold comfort.

"He'll be all right," Poppy reassured her. "Eclipse is smart."

Lunar stared between the two women, noting the

way they comforted each other and softened their words. It was a strange human phenomenon.

Poppy had the fire crackling to life, warm light pushing back the shadows. She turned to Lunar with a slight frown. She pointed at the countertop. "Your skin-suit was in my bag, but it looks completely deteriorated."

Lunar studied the useless garment. It would no longer help to hide him.

"I am optimal in darkness," Lunar said. The star patterns within his shadow essence emanated more brightly here, away from the harsh lights of civilization. "This environment suits my needs."

Poppy's expression softened, that particular look she got when observing his true nature. Part wonder, part attraction, part something deeper he couldn't quite categorize.

"We should establish a watch rotation," Lunar continued, forcing himself to focus on necessities. "Their search pattern will expand once they lose our trail."

"I'll take first watch," Rowan said immediately. "I won't be able to sleep anyway."

Lunar started to say that the humans should rest first, but Poppy caught his eye and shook her head slightly. She came close, touching his arm as she said quietly, "Rowan needs the distraction. Even if she could fall asleep, it would bring only nightmares of what would happen to Eclipse if Milano captures him. If it were us, I wouldn't be able to sleep knowing you were out there."

"I will patrol the perimeter," Lunar offered.

Poppy's hand on his arm stopped him from moving toward the door. Even through his shadow form, her touch created those familiar ripples of sensation.

"Be careful," she said softly. "Milano might have infrared scanners or other tech we don't know about. Assume nothing is safe."

"I will return within the Earth hour," he assured her, allowing his fingers to briefly intertwine with hers. The connection sent star patterns swirling through his form, a reaction he no longer tried to suppress. He liked the way her eyes followed them.

Outside, the desert night embraced him, and he felt like he was home. Though Earth's darkness lacked the absolute quality of the Lunaris Zone, it offered sufficient shadow for his needs. He moved through the canyon like flowing ink, checking approach routes and noting defensive positions. In the freedom of night, he found himself drifting, his mind straying from his purpose as his thoughts turned back to Poppy.

Poppy.

He had never encountered a being so... Poppy. There were no adequate human words to describe her. The earthlings had not mastered a language that could encompass everything she represented. Poppy was like the perfect blend of shadows shifting across the distant landscape, an endless night of beauty. She was the dot of stars, steady and fixed in the night sky to guide him where he needed to go.

The humans seemed to grasp a concept better than his kind. They called it love. But even that word didn't seem big enough to carry the full weight of what it defined.

Poppy.

Love.

He wanted to get back to her, to be in her orbit.

His shadow senses detected no immediate threats, but the situation remained precarious. Milano had demonstrated resources beyond standard Earth military capabilities. They would not abandon their hunt easily.

As he circled back toward the cabin, Lunar

found himself considering futures he'd never imagined. His mission parameters had become irrelevant the moment Poppy had seen through his shadow concealment.

The shadow territories needed his intelligence about Earth. The brewing conflict on Zorveya demanded every tactical advantage. Yet standing here in Earth's darkness, sensing Poppy's warm presence in the cabin ahead, Lunar felt the certainties of his existence fragmenting. Earth no longer felt like a place to be used. It was no longer a distant objective. These humans deserved more than to be a military advantage for a distant planet.

When he returned to the cabin, he found Rowan positioned by the window. Eclipse's stone still glowed faintly in her open hand, like she was trying to decipher messages from it. Poppy had made a meal out of Mack's supplies.

"Anything?" Poppy asked as he entered. She gestured to the table where a bowl of food waited.

"No immediate threats," Lunar reported. "But we should not become complacent."

Flowing through the night had greatly increased his energy levels, and he did not require the food for substance, but still, he came to sit beside her.

"Rowan, if you're hungry..." Poppy called to her friend.

They ate in relative silence. Rowan picked at her food, her attention clearly elsewhere. The weight of unspoken fears filled the small space. Poppy kept glancing at Lunar, questions evident in her expression but unvoiced.

"I need some air." Rowan stood abruptly, moving toward the door. "I'll maintain watch from outside."

"The temperature is dropping," Poppy cautioned. "At least take the blanket from the cot."

Rowan accepted the advice with a grateful nod and slipped outside, Eclipse's stone clutched against her chest like a talisman.

Alone with Poppy, Lunar felt the atmosphere shift. The pretense of tactical discussion fell away, leaving only the connection that hummed between them like a living thing.

"We have to find out what happened to him. She won't survive losing him," Poppy said quietly, staring at the closed door. "The way she holds that stone... It's like that is the only thing keeping her together."

"Eclipse is resourceful," Lunar replied, though the words felt hollow. "If anyone can survive Milano's interrogation, it would be him."

"So you think Milano has him for sure?" Poppy asked. "Maybe he's hiding in the cave?"

Lunar reached out to take her hand. "He would have come to us if he could have. He would have followed my signature. The more time that passes, the more likely it is that he was captured. I can't feel him in the night."

Poppy turned to face him fully, firelight dancing across her features. "And if Galaxy Brides comes back for you? What then? Will you go home with Solar?"

That was the very question he'd been avoiding. It hung between them like a physical presence. Lunar found himself moving closer, drawn by forces that had nothing to do with shadow manipulation or tactical advantage.

"My mission parameters have become complicated," he admitted.

"Because of me?" Poppy asked, though her tone suggested she already knew the answer.

"Because of what you represent," Lunar clarified, reaching out to trace the curve of her cheek with shadowy fingers. "A possibility I had not considered. A future that diverges from everything I was created to be."

Damn these Earth words. He couldn't find the right ones to explain.

Poppy leaned into his touch, her warmth creating those familiar patterns where their energies met. "You were created to be a shadow operative. But maybe you can choose to be something more."

"Choice," Lunar repeated, testing the word. "Shadow-dwellers are not encouraged to embrace such concepts."

"Yet here you are," Poppy said softly, "making choices every moment you stay with me."

The truth of her words resonated through his being. Each moment since their first encounter had been a choice, small divergences from his programmed path that had led him here, to this cabin, to this woman who saw through darkness as easily as breathing.

"I am compromised," Lunar concluded, the admission both liberating and terrifying. "My objectivity regarding Earth no longer exists. By every measure of shadow operative protocols, I have failed."

He hadn't even been logging his mission reports to take home.

Poppy moved closer, her hand finding his in the dancing firelight. "Or maybe you've succeeded in ways you didn't expect. Maybe connection is worth more than intelligence gathering."

"A romantic perspective," Lunar observed.

"A human perspective," Poppy corrected. "Though I'm starting to think it's not just a human thing. Solar and Dani, Eclipse and Rowan, you and me... There's something about these connections that transcends species. I have to believe there was some kind of fate that brought you three here at this time to meet us. There's a power in the universe greater than all of us. It drew our energies together. What are the odds that we would find each other so quickly, so assuredly?"

Lunar considered this, analyzing the patterns that had emerged. Three Zorveyan representatives, each finding unexpected resonance with Earth females. Statistically improbable unless some deeper meaning existed.

"You may be correct," he said. "The resonance between us suggests factors beyond simple attraction. Your shadow sensitivity, in particular, indicates possible genetic variations that—"

Poppy silenced him with a kiss, her lips warm against his cool. The familiar circuit of energy estab-lished itself instantly, star patterns accelerating within his darkness as her warmth flowed into him.

When they parted, her smile carried a gentle amusement. "You're overthinking again."

"Analysis is my nature," Lunar defended, though he felt his clinical perspective dissolving under her touch.

"Your nature is changing," Poppy observed. "I can feel it in your energy. The patterns are different than when we first met. More complex. More..."

"Human?" Lunar suggested with what might have been irony.

"More open," Poppy corrected. "Like shadows at the edge of dawn, when they start to soften and blend instead of standing in sharp relief."

The poetic description sparked something in Lunar's consciousness, a recognition that Poppy understood his nature in ways that even other shadow-dwellers might not. She saw not only the darkness but the subtle variations within it, the beauty in the absence of light.

A soft knock interrupted them. Rowan peered inside the open door, her face drawn with exhaustion despite her earlier insistence on taking watch.

"You should rest," Poppy told her gently. "Lunar and I can handle the watch."

Rowan hesitated, clearly torn between exhaustion and the need to remain vigilant for any news of

Eclipse. Finally, fatigue won. She moved to the cot, still clutching the energy stone.

"Wake me if anything changes," she said, her voice thick with unshed tears. "He's out there. Alone."

"I know. We will," Poppy promised.

As Rowan settled onto the narrow cot, Lunar and Poppy moved outside into the desert night. The temperature had dropped significantly, but Poppy seemed unbothered.

"I can only imagine what she's feeling," Poppy whispered. "The idea of a missing loved one is probably one of the worst feelings in the world. The not knowing."

They found a natural shelter in the rocks above the cabin, a position that offered clear sightlines while remaining concealed. Poppy settled against a smooth boulder, and Lunar flowed around her, his shadow form providing both warmth and protection.

"How long do you think we can hide here?" Poppy asked after a while, her voice barely above a whisper.

"Unknown," Lunar admitted. "Milano's resources appear extensive. But this location offers significant tactical advantages."

"That's not what I meant," Poppy said softly.

"How long before Galaxy Brides returns? How long before you have to choose between duty and...?" She gave a helpless gesture. "Between duty and us?"

The question pierced through his defenses more effectively than any weapon. Lunar found himself tightening his protective embrace, as if he could shield them both from the inevitable.

"I don't know," he answered at length. He hoped for more time than duty would dictate.

Poppy turned in his arms. Her eyes found his. "Whatever time we have, I want to spend it without regrets. Without holding back because of what might come."

"A dangerous philosophy," Lunar observed, even as he felt himself drawn to it.

"The only one worth living by," Poppy countered. "Especially now, when everything feels balanced on a knife's edge."

She was right, of course. He found she understood these things better than he. Their situation was precarious, their future uncertain. Logic dictated maintaining emotional distance and preparing for their inevitable separation. But logic had failed him the moment she'd placed that first shadow stone at his feet.

"Then we proceed without reservation," Lunar

decided, surprising himself with the conviction in his voice. "Whatever time remains, we face it together."

Poppy's smile illuminated the darkness more effectively than any star.

"Together," she agreed, sealing the promise with another kiss that sent shadow and warmth spiraling between them.

The passion that hummed between them built like static electricity before a storm. Lunar's essence swirled with increasing intensity, his star patterns accelerating as Poppy's warmth called to him.

"I want to feel you again," Poppy whispered, turning in his embrace.

Her hands traced over his darkness, sending ripples of sensation wherever she touched. The desert night cradled them in perfect privacy, red rocks rising around their hidden alcove like ancient guardians. Lunar responded by letting his shadow form flow over her exposed skin like cool silk, each point of contact creating those familiar circuits of energy between them.

Poppy shivered as she pulled her shirt over her head, exposing herself to the night air. Lunar's shadow essence caressed her breasts, drawing a gasp as his cooler darkness met warm, soft flesh. His touch was everywhere at once, ghosting across her nipples, trailing down her stomach, sliding along her thighs as she shed the rest of her clothing.

She made tiny noises that called to something deep inside. When he solidified partially to take her breast in his mouth, the contrast of his tongue against her heated skin made her arch against him.

"You fascinate me," she whispered.

Star patterns swirled faster within his form as her hands explored his body, finding him solid where she needed him to be. Her hands moved over him and through him.

"Please," she breathed as his fingers slid between her thighs, touching her in the way he had learned she liked. He found her wet, a human signal that she was ready for him. The star patterns within his darkness pulsed in response to her desire.

He molded his form against her, his essence pushing forward to fill her body the way she wanted. Lunar groaned, the sound resonating through his entire being as her inner muscles gripped him. He sent pulses of his energy into her, growing himself inside her tight depths.

"I very much enjoy your wet pleasure port," he admitted, pushing himself deeper and stretching wider.

Poppy gave a small giggle before gasping. "I very much enjoy you in my pleasure port."

They moved together in the darkness, finding a wiggling rhythm that built like an approaching storm. Lunar's shadow essence enveloped her completely while maintaining that exquisite friction where their bodies joined. Each thrust sent waves of ecstasy through their connected energies.

She cried out in pleasure as he felt a spark along her nerve endings where they merged. The faster he pulsed, the more she writhed. Her legs wrapped around him, and she grabbed his hips to pull him tighter.

Poppy's ability to channel shadow frequencies amplified every sensation. They were connected in a way that should not be possible. He felt her not just physically but energetically. He felt her desire, her pleasure, her growing need that resonated through his being. Her passion fed back into him, creating loops of shared sensation that spiraled higher and higher.

When release finally claimed them, it was a cosmic release. Poppy's orgasm triggered Lunar's, and their combined energies exploded outward like a supernova, creating a burst of soft blue light. For an endless moment, they were one being, shadow and human perfectly balanced in crystalline pleasure. The star patterns within Lunar's form blazed so brightly they illuminated the night around them before settling back into gentle swirls.

Afterward, they remained entangled, Poppy's warmth wrapped in his protective darkness. He kept his essence partially inside her, unwilling to fully separate. The connection between them was stronger than ever, and he felt as if a permanent bridge had been forged between their energies.

"I love you," Poppy whispered into the darkness. "Whatever comes next, whatever choices we have to make, I want you to know that won't change."

Lunar tightened his embrace.

"You have altered me in ways that cannot be undone," he replied. "My darkness will always resonate with your light."

He again wished Earth had given him better words to tell her how he felt.

The desert stretched endlessly around them, keeping its secrets while they carved out their own small sanctuary in the shadow of the rocks. They stayed that way until dawn began to paint the eastern sky in shades of gray and pink, grasping every moment of connection while they could.

Lunar felt the familiar threat of impending

daylight. Soon he would need to retreat to the cabin's shadows. But for just a moment longer, he held Poppy close, memorizing the feel of her warmth against his darkness, storing each sensation against an uncertain future.

Whatever came next—*Milano, Galaxy Brides, or choices he couldn't yet fathom*—this moment was theirs. And in the end, perhaps that was all anyone could ask for, a perfect moment of connection in a universe full of shadows and light.

12

POPPY WOKE TO SUNLIGHT STREAMING THROUGH the cabin's single window onto her face. For a moment, she was disoriented. Where was Lunar? Then she felt his cool presence behind her, his shadow form pressed against the darkest corner of the narrow cot. Even in sleep, he instinctively avoided direct light.

She carefully extricated herself, not wanting to disturb him. The wood stove had burned down to embers overnight, leaving the cabin chilly. Rowan sat vigil by the window, still clutching Eclipse's energy stone. She'd fashioned a necklace out of it, hanging it around her neck in a leather pouch. From her posture, Poppy doubted she'd slept at all.

"Any change?" Poppy asked softly, though she already knew the answer.

Rowan shook her head. "The stone's energy feels weaker today. What if..." Her voice cracked. "What if that means he's...?"

"He's alive," Poppy said firmly, moving to stoke the fire. She couldn't bear to see her friend's pain. "Eclipse is too stubborn to give up. And Milano needs him alive. They wouldn't risk harming their only captive alien."

The words felt hollow even as she said them. What did they really know about Milano's intentions? The corporation had chased them across the desert with military precision, using technology that shouldn't exist on Earth. The implications were terrifying if she let herself think about them too deeply.

A soft whirring sound interrupted her thoughts. Something that looked like a cross between a hummingbird and a metal dragonfly hovered outside the window.

"Lunar," she called sharply, recognizing possible alien tech. "Rowan, get away from the window!"

The shadows in the corner coalesced instantly into his more defined form.

"Galaxy Brides messenger drone," he said, not

appearing worried as he moved to examine it. "Primitive but functional."

"Do they have Eclipse?" Rowan demanded, rushing toward the door to let the dragonfly drone inside.

Lunar went to the drone and lifted his hand. Dark swirls left his hand to surround the tech. "I'll tell them we are safe in this cabin and that we think Milano has captured Eclipse in the caves. I'll ask them to look for his energy signatures from their location in space to see if they can track him."

"Yes, do that." Rowan let loose an eager breath.

"It is done," he stated.

"And...?" Rowan begged.

As if responding to them, the drone projected a flickering hologram of Bob and Gary's oversized heads floating in the cabin's dim interior. Their skinsuits looked even worse than before.

Or maybe the sickly yellow was just their actual skin. Poppy couldn't be sure as she stared at the transparent image.

"Greetings valued clients," Gary's voice crackled through static. "We are processing your request to rescue Eclipse. Don't you worry. We're on the case. Solar and Dani are on board and safe. We're pleased to inform you that a new extraction window has been calculated. Fourteen Earth days from now, we can facilitate your return journey. The coordinates will be transmitted separately to avoid Milano's detection systems."

Poppy's heart clenched. Fourteen days. Two weeks until she might lose Lunar forever.

The dragonfly began sputtering and spinning, taking Bob and Gary's image with it as they projected around the room in dizzying circles.

"Stay where you are. Do not attempt to deviate from the scheduled window," Bob's garbled voice added. "Harris will come for you. The energy matrices are very delicate. One wrong move and you could end up scattered across multiple dimensions. The company's contracts you signed don't cover dimensional scattering."

The hologram flickered out, leaving them in stunned silence. The dragonfly exploded like a fire-cracker and dropped to the floor in flames. Poppy instantly stomped it to put out the fire.

Fourteen days. The countdown had begun.

"But what about Eclipse?" Rowan demanded into the silence, yelling down at the exploded device on the floor like it could still transmit her worry. "On the case? Processing our request to rescue Eclipse? What the hell does that mean? That's not an answer!"

Poppy nudged the smoking remains of the drag-onfly drone with her toe. Even their messenger tech was unreliable. She looked up at the ceiling, imagining what their spaceship must look like. Was it even safe for travel? How could they trust Galaxy Brides with extraction when they couldn't even make a drone that didn't explode?

"Processing the request has to mean they're doing something about it," Poppy said, trying to sound optimistic. "At least we know Solar and Dani made it safely. They won't let Galaxy Brides drop the ball on this, Rowan. We're going to find him. I promise, no one is leaving without him."

Leaving. The word was meant to comfort her friend, but it caused a deep pang of agony in Poppy's chest. She looked at Lunar, trying not to let the pain overtake her.

Fourteen days.

It wasn't enough time.

Lunar moved to examine the drone's remains. His shadow essence flowed around the charred metal. "The transmission originated from high orbit."

"They can find Eclipse from up there?" Rowan clutched the energy stone tighter. "There has to be something more we can do. We can't just sit here for two weeks while Milano..." She trailed off, as if unable to finish saying the thought out loud. "Please, Lunar. I can't lose him."

"I do not feel he is lost," Lunar said. He awkwardly patted Rowan's shoulder.

Rowan took the small comfort and nodded. She stared at the destroyed drone like it could give her answers.

Poppy's stomach growled, reminding her they needed to think about practical matters too. She headed to the shelves where Mack kept his supplies. "We need breakfast. Then we can figure out our next move."

"I'm not hungry," Rowan answered.

Poppy pulled down cans of beans and fruit cocktail. It wasn't exactly a gourmet meal, but it would keep them going. As she worked to heat the beans over the wood stove, her mind raced through possibilities. They had two weeks. Two weeks to find Eclipse, two weeks until the extraction window, two weeks until...

She glanced at Lunar, who had positioned himself in the shadows near the door. Two weeks until she might lose him forever. The thought made her hands shake as she stirred the beans.

She wanted to beg him to stay.

Maybe she should beg him to take her with him.

Outside, a storm was brewing as if to give a visual presence to what they were feeling. Dark clouds gathered over the canyon, promising the kind of sudden deluge that could turn desert washes into raging rivers within minutes. At least the weather would help keep Milano's helicopters grounded even as it trapped them indoors.

As she watched the storm build, Poppy couldn't shake the feeling that it was an omen. Changes were coming, whether they were ready or not.

13

POPPY WOKE IN DARKNESS, HER BODY STIFF FROM sleeping on the cabin floor. She'd insisted Rowan take the cot, hoping her friend might finally get some real rest. The first hints of pre-dawn light filtered through the curtains, casting weird shadows across the room.

Something felt wrong.

She sat up slowly, letting her eyes adjust. Lunar's presence emanated from the darkest corner, but Rowan's cot was empty. A hastily scrawled note lay abandoned on the thin mattress.

Her heart sank as she read the words, *"Gone to find Eclipse. Milano has him. Don't follow. Stay hidden. I'll be back."*

"No, no, no..." Poppy scrambled to the window, already knowing what she'd find. The jeep was gone.

"Lunar!" She turned to where his shadow form coalesced into a more solid shape. "Rowan's gone. She took the jeep."

"I know," he said calmly. "I heard her leave an hour ago."

"What? And you didn't stop her?" Poppy ran out the front door and stared at the rough dirt road leading away from the cabin. Her friend was out there alone, driving straight into Milano's grasp.

Dammit, Rowan!

Poppy went back into the cabin to check their supplies. Almost everything seemed untouched. Rowan had only taken water and the basic emergency kit they always kept in the vehicle. Did that mean she was planning on coming back soon? What if he jeep stopped and Rowan got stranded without enough food or water?

"What was she thinking?" Poppy whispered to herself, trying to figure out what to do.

"The stone changed," Lunar said. His darkness swirled. "Its energy signature became different from yesterday."

"Different how?" Poppy asked.

"Eclipse started communicating through it," Lunar said, very matter-of-fact. "Somehow, his energy signature managed to reach her. He's talking to her. They have a deep connection."

"We have to go after her." Poppy moved to go back outside.

"No." Lunar's form solidified as he moved to keep her from leaving. "Milano's forces are specifically equipped to detect our energy signatures. If I leave this location, I will draw them straight to her. I will not risk her life or Eclipse's. I trust that if he called her, he has a plan. I must trust that plan."

"But we can't just let her go alone." She desperately wanted to make him understand. "This is not how we do things on Earth."

"It appears to be how Rowan does things. She made a tactical choice," Lunar stated, though Poppy could hear the strain in his voice. "By going alone, she maintains optimal stealth parameters. My presence would only endanger them both."

"You said that already." Poppy frowned. He was right, damn him.

"I was not sure you heard it," he answered. "You seem panicked, and I wish to stop that."

There were so many things she liked about Lunar, but his constant calmness and logic weren't always one of them.

Poppy sank onto the empty cot. "So we just, what? Wait?"

She didn't want to wait. They'd been in the cabin for days. It felt like all they were doing was waiting.

"For now," Lunar confirmed. His shadow essence enveloped her shoulders in comfort. "Rowan has proven remarkably capable. And if Eclipse is communicating through the stone, he will guide her. We must trust them."

Outside, the sun began to rise over the canyon rim, painting the rocks in shades of blood and fire. It felt like a bad omen. Somewhere out there, her friend raced toward danger, following the call of an alien energy stone.

"I can't believe she just left." Poppy paced the small cabin. Three days of waiting had clearly been too much for Rowan. "She could have at least woken me up. Told me she was leaving."

"She knew you would try to stop her," Lunar observed. "Or insist on going with her."

He was right. Of course, he was right. Poppy would have never let Rowan go alone into danger.

The morning dragged by with agonizing slowness. She felt Lunar watching her, and his essence touched her when she neared the shadows. Poppy tried to keep busy, stoking the fire, checking their dwindling supplies, and watching the road through gaps in the curtains. But her mind stayed on Rowan. Was she okay? Had she found Eclipse? Had Milano captured her too?

"You're projecting anxiety," Lunar said, interrupting her umpteenth pace around the cabin. "It disrupts the shadow frequencies."

"Sorry, my concern is inconvenient," Poppy snapped, then immediately regretted it. "I just... I hate this. Sitting here. Waiting. Not knowing."

"I understand." Lunar's form rippled. "Rowan is intelligent. She will avoid main routes. Does this comfort you?"

Poppy arched a brow and took a deep breath. At least he was trying. "Yeah, thanks, Lunar."

Lunar melted into the shadows. She felt him but didn't see him. Another hour crawled by, or at least it felt like an hour. She couldn't be sure. She concentrated on the sound of her feet in the silence.

"Do you think..." she started, then hesitated.

"Yes?" Lunar answered from the darkness.

"Do you think they really have a connection where they can feel each other over the distance? Eclipse and Rowan?"

"Yes."

"And Solar and Dani?"

"I would assume. Solarians' communication is much louder, but they do have the ability to connect."

Poppy buried a small laugh at the dig against Solar. "Do you think some kind of cosmic fate brought you three here to find us? I mean, when I think of the odds..."

Lunar was quiet for a long moment. "Shadow operatives do not typically believe in fate. But I have observed that the resonance between human and Zorveyan energy signatures defies statistical probability."

Poppy smiled despite her worry. Trust Lunar to turn cosmic destiny into a math problem.

The smile faded as the sound of helicopters drifted down from above.

"They're getting closer," she said, hurrying to the window.

"That craft sounds different than the ones Milano sent before. Don't worry, the mineral composition of Mack's cabin roof continues to shield us," Lunar assured her. "They cannot detect my presence from above."

The helicopter might have nothing to do with Milano. It could be a medical flight or a desert tour. The thought didn't make her feel better.

Poppy took a deep breath and stepped back

from the window as the helicopter flew away from their location. Hiding in fear sucked. But what came next would be even worse. Galaxy Brides would extract Lunar in less than two weeks. And when that time came, would she be strong enough to let him go?

The day crawled on, each second marked by Poppy's footsteps as she paced. She kept mentally calculating how far Rowan might have gotten, what routes she might have taken.

"You should eat something," Lunar suggested.

"Not hungry." She knew she was being difficult, but she couldn't help it. The inaction was driving her crazy.

A helicopter passed particularly close overhead. Poppy froze, holding her breath until the sound faded.

"I hate this," she whispered. "I know why she did it, but I just feel so useless."

Lunar's shadow form moved closer, cool tendrils of darkness brushing her arm in what she'd come to recognize as a comforting gesture. "Your presence here is not useless. You provide shelter. Safety."

"Great. I'm a really good hideout." She immediately regretted the sarcasm when his darkness pulled back slightly. "I didn't mean... I know we need to stay hidden. I know you being seen would only make things worse."

"My energy levels are now optimal. Come against me," he said, reaching to pull her closer. "I feel as if I need to hold you."

Poppy instantly went into his embrace. His touch calmed her, and she felt as if she could breathe easier. His energy hummed over her, realigning her tension so her thoughts became less frantic. Is this how he managed to remain so steady and calm?

She leaned into his embrace, and time seemed to stand still. Her mind drifted as if carried into a dream. They didn't move, but she felt the electricity of his touch thrumming through her like a current. Her nerves tingled as if they absorbed him into her body.

"I will take your tension from you," he said.

She inhaled sharply. Part of him flowed inside of her like invisible smoke. He filled her lungs and curled lower until the sensation tickled her sex. Pure desire unfolded in the stillness. He moved beneath her clothes without undressing her. His body fluctuated between ethereal and solid forms. His kiss moved along her cheek like a fine mist before exploding all over her body at once.

Then his essence crept between her legs and

expanded up to fill her even as she remained clothed. His coolness warmed as he swirled inside her. The pressure tingled, and she rocked against him as he held her upright. Her knees weakened as she climaxed, trying to grab hold of his changing form.

As the tremors eased, she realized her feet were no longer touching the floor. She looked down to see that they hovered over the ground. Lunar slowly lowered her.

"I carry the feelings for you," he said when he released her.

Poppy wasn't sure what he meant by that, but assumed he referred to the anxiety he took from her with his contact. "Thanks."

She had no concept of time when he held her, but now she saw the sun had begun to set, casting the canyon in deep shadows.

"Do you think Rowan found him?" Poppy asked quietly.

"If Eclipse communicated through the stone, then yes," Lunar replied. "He would not risk contact unless he had a way to guide her."

Poppy nodded, trying to take comfort in that logic. "I just hope they're both okay."

She settled onto the cot, exhausted from worry

and tension. Lunar's shadow essence swirled around her like a protective cloak.

"Rest," he suggested, running a ghost of a hand over her eyes. "I will maintain watch."

A soft whirring sound broke the silence. Another mechanical dragonfly hovered outside their window, this one slightly less battered than the previous messenger. It flew against the window, bouncing on the glass as it tried to get inside.

"Another one?" Poppy moved toward the window, but Lunar's shadow essence held her back. "They might have information about Rowan."

"Allow me to verify," he said, extending tendrils of darkness to examine the drone. "It appears to be from Galaxy Brides."

He opened the door to let it inside.

The drone projected Bob and Gary's disembodied heads into the cabin. Their fake skin looked even worse than before, hanging off their yellow flesh and rolling away from their eyes. The disguises wouldn't fool a toddler.

"Emergency extraction protocols initiated," Bob announced without preamble. "Maintain position at current coordinates. Extraction team will come to you."

"What about Eclipse?" Poppy demanded. "Have you found him?"

"So-Sol-uh-Sola..." Gary stuttered. " No. I can't say more. Situation developing. Stay where you are. Harris will come when the time is right. Be ready."

The transmission cut off abruptly as the drone sparked and went dark, dropping to the floor with a sad little *thunk*.

"At least this one didn't explode," Poppy observed dryly.

She spoke too soon. The drone sparked and popped like a firecracker before letting off a stream of smoke.

"What do you think they mean by soon?" A wave of sadness washed over her. They were supposed to have more time.

Lunar absorbed the drone's remains into his shadow essence. "I believe soon is defined as happening after a short time."

"I know what soon means, I just don't know what they mean when they say it," Poppy insisted. "A week? A day? Hours?"

Lunar would not meet her gaze. "I would guess they mean closer to the last option. Otherwise, they would have given the time by days or weeks."

Poppy sank onto the cot, exhaustion catching up

with her, but she was too emotional to rest. She buried her head in her hands and took a deep breath. Lunar's cool darkness enveloped her like a protective cloak to soothe her thoughts.

"Rest," he suggested. "I will maintain watch."

"I can't," she denied, shaking her head.

His energy came over her in waves, urging her to stop fighting the need to sleep.

"Wake me if anything changes?" Poppy mumbled. Whatever happened next, at least they weren't facing it alone.

"Of course," he whispered. "Rest."

14

LUNAR DETECTED APPROACHING ENERGY signatures. The familiar twilight resonance was dangerously unstable, accompanied by Milano's pursuing aircraft.

He materialized near the window where Poppy dozed and touched her arm to wake her gently. He had used his energy to coax her to sleep. It was for the best. He had not liked the accelerated vitals he perceived when he'd touched her. Now he pulled that energy back to let her wake up. "Poppy. Something's coming."

She gave a small moan as she fought to open her eyes.

Through gaps in the curtains, he watched two forms emerge from the darkness. Eclipse and Rowan.

Eclipse flickered with weakening twilight energy, while Rowan was distinctly human. His fellow Zorveyan's essence streamed behind them like Earth's aurora, but the pattern was wrong, scattered.

What had Milano done to him?

They tumbled from the air at the cabin's perimeter, Eclipse's form barely maintaining cohesion as Rowan rolled free.

"Eclipse!" Rowan's cry carried raw fear as she scrambled across the ground to reach him.

Lunar moved swiftly to them, his shadow essence stretching over to Eclipse's failing twilight energy. The damage was severe, worse than he'd anticipated. Eclipse's normally stable twilight field fluctuated wildly, threatening to dissipate completely.

"He is severely depleted," Lunar observed, carefully modulating his tone to hide his concern. He tried to infuse his energy into Eclipse. It helped steady him a little. But he'd used a lot of his reserves to calm Poppy and force her to rest.

"Help him," Rowan pleaded as helicopter searchlights swept closer.

"Inside," Lunar ordered, expanding his shadow form to help gather Eclipse's scattered essence. "The structure is shielded."

Together, they brought Eclipse into the cabin.

Lunar's shadow essence cradled the failing twilight energy, providing structure where Eclipse's form threatened to dissolve completely. He'd never seen the diplomat so damaged. In fact, he couldn't remember seeing anyone on his homeworld this damaged.

"What happened to him?" Poppy demanded, locking the door. She still looked sleepy and a little disconcerted as she smoothed back her hair.

"Milano," Rowan answered. "They had him in some kind of energy containment. He broke free but used everything he had to get us here."

Lunar sensed Eclipse's essence dispersing even more, with waves of agony spreading through the twilight field. This was more than mere depletion. Milano had somehow destabilized Eclipse's energy patterns at a fundamental level.

"His cohesion is failing," Lunar stated, carefully regulating his own shadow energy to avoid overwhelming Eclipse's weakened state. "He requires energy replenishment."

They moved Eclipse to the cot while Poppy drew heavy curtains over the windows. She draped a purple rag over the single lamp, creating an artificial twilight that might help stabilize their friend.

Rowan knelt beside Eclipse's fluctuating form

and tried to touch him, as if pushing his energy back into his body. "What are we going to do?

"After you left, Galaxy Brides contacted Lunar again." Poppy's voice was tight, and he felt her tension. He hated it when she felt sad or scared. "They said they would pick us up for an emergency extraction. Soon."

Lunar detected a shift in Eclipse's failing energy as he attempted to speak. The diplomat's essence scattered with the effort, but Rowan seemed to understand the garbled words.

"He's trying to tell us something," she said. "Something about communications."

Lunar listened for what she heard, but only picked up faint sounds coming from Eclipse.

Through their connection, Rowan translated Eclipse's fragmented warning, "Milano intercepted Galaxy Brides' communications. They know about the extraction point."

Lunar's shadow essence grew darker as the implications became clearer. He absorbed more light from the room and tried to filter it to Eclipse. "That must be why Gary changed their original fourteen-day plan."

"We were supposed to have more time," Poppy said.

"When we were training for Earth on the ship, Galaxy Brides mentioned a possible emergency protocol if Earth threats discovered our location." Lunar shifted uncomfortably. "They deliberately kept details vague in case one of us was compromised."

Through their energy resonance, Lunar felt Eclipse struggling to convey more information. Rowan translated again, "Tonight? You're leaving tonight?"

The shortened timeline's harsh reality impacted Lunar on a physical level. Psychological pain rippled through him at the thought of leaving. "Milano's pursuit has forced Galaxy Brides to accelerate their timeline. They cannot risk waiting."

Helicopter rotors grew louder outside. Lunar extended his senses, analyzing the threat pattern. Three aircraft and a coordinated search grid. Milano was closing in.

"I count three helicopters circling the area," Poppy confirmed from the window.

Eclipse tried to rise, but his essence scattered further. Lunar moved to the cabin's center, extending his shadow field to reinforce the natural shielding. "The protection remains intact. Milano's scanners cannot penetrate the mineral composition of the roof. As long as we're careful, they won't find us."

Eclipse stabilized in the artificial twilight and shared more fragments of intelligence through Rowan. Milano had encountered other aliens. They were preparing for what they called an inevitable expansion. They wanted to weaponize alien technology.

"They don't just want to study us," Rowan summarized. "They want to weaponize alien technology. Prepare Earth for some kind of interstellar conflict."

"Typical primitive species paranoia," Lunar said, though the tactical implications troubled him deeply.

"Is it paranoia if there really are hostile aliens?" Poppy pressed her face to the glass to look outside. He felt an emotional barrier forming between them and did not like it.

It could be argued that Earthlings were the hostile aliens in this scenario, but he refrained. Before Lunar could respond, Eclipse projected another urgent warning through Rowan. Milano knew the extraction coordinates. They were setting a trap.

Lunar's essence darkened further as options narrowed. "This complicates matters. Galaxy Brides cannot be notified. Any transmission might be intercepted."

"So what do we do?" Poppy asked. "We can't just walk into an ambush, but we can't miss the extraction either."

Through the weakening twilight field, Eclipse tried to suggest an alternative extraction location, but it was tactically illogical. He wasn't making much sense. The diplomat's essence flickered as exhaustion claimed him.

Lunar frowned as Eclipse drifted into a recovery state. Rowan maintained physical contact as if she could anchor his dispersed essence through touch alone. Their bond's effectiveness was unmistakable.

Time felt compressed as they planned in whispers. Eclipse slowly continued to recover. Poppy wore headphones as she tried to listen to a radio for human air traffic chatter. Rowan collapsed in pure exhaustion, falling asleep next to Eclipse. When the diplomat next achieved consciousness, hours had passed.

"You recover quickly for one so damaged." Lunar materialized from his vigil in the corner.

Eclipse glanced at Rowan but didn't wake up. Lunar kept his voice low so as not to disturb the woman as she slept.

He leaned into Eclipse. The diplomat didn't speak with human words, but he heard his voice in his head through their essence. Their whispered conversation laid bare the brutal mathematics of survival. They had about four hours before they would be forced to run. Milano's forces were drawing closer with each passing minute. Lunar felt the weight of unspoken choices pressing against him. His mission demanded a return to Zorveya. The shadow territories needed to be warned of Milano's long term plans. Yet every time he looked at Poppy, his carefully constructed logic threatened to dissolve.

She had her hands over the headphones while she looked out of the window, scanning the darkness for threats, unaware that she represented his greatest tactical vulnerability. His shadow essence reached for her unconsciously, even as his mind calculated the increasing probability that he would not be able to leave when Harris' extraction window opened.

Rowan yawned and opened her eyes. Blinking to awareness, she turned to look at Eclipse. "You're better."

Lunar withdrew to let them speak. He moved to be near Poppy. Before he could touch her shoulder, a sharp knock interrupted them. Poppy jerked and pulled off the headphones.

Lunar's essence immediately expanded, defensive protocols engaging as he sensed a familiar energy signature beyond the door. "Galaxy Alien Mail Order Brides."

Poppy's hand raised in warning. "Wait. How do you know it's Galaxy Brides? We should be careful. It could be a trap."

"I don't think Milano would knock on the door," Rowan reasoned.

Lunar extended his senses through the door's material, confirming the visitor's identity before opening it to reveal Harris in his partially scorched business suit.

The trainee's appearance shattered what remained of their sanctuary. "Emergency extraction protocol enacted. Location discovered. Milano forces are converging. Must depart immediately."

At least the alien's translator finally seemed to be working.

Time had run out. They would have to choose. Now.

Harris kept talking. His huge eyes blinked rapidly. Lunar couldn't concentrate on the rambling words. His attention kept trying to focus on Poppy. She stared at him, as if waiting for him to say something. But what could he tell her? His people needed him to go. He wanted to stay.

Duty. Desire. The two behaviors did not align.

Lunar exchanged a look with Eclipse, noting how the diplomat's essence still wavered dangerously, like a candle flame flickering in the wind. Whatever Milano had done to him had fundamentally destabilized his energy.

"Transport waiting one kilometer north. Must hurry," Harris said, already backing toward the door.

Eclipse attempted to gather his essence to move, but Lunar saw him falter, his form briefly dispersing into wisps of purple-blue light before reconsolidating. Rowan immediately steadied him, her hand instinctively finding the sturdiest part of his wavering form.

"Can you make it?" Rowan asked.

Eclipse nodded in the affirmative.

Poppy gathered supplies. Lunar watched her hands, those delicate human appendages that had traced patterns through his darkness, that had somehow touched parts of his being no physical contact should reach. Even now, he felt her mark on him. She'd altered his genetic makeup.

He couldn't help analyzing her. Poppy's movements were quick but precise, grabbing only what they truly needed. Adaptable. Resourceful. Qualities he had come to admire in her species.

He pulled Harris aside while the others prepared, his shadow essence enveloping them both for privacy. "Explain the extraction parameters."

The trainee's rambling explanation confirmed what he'd suspected. The dimensional bridge Galaxy Brides used required balanced energy signatures— *light, shadow, and twilight*. It could not accept human lifeforms, at least not safely. Poppy would not be coming.

"Dimensional fold becomes black hole-adjacent phenomenon," Harris squeaked, his translator struggling with the concept. "Ship waiting in orbit would be... scattered. Non-recoverable."

Solar. Dani. The extraction vessel. All of them lost.

Lunar retracted his shadow essence, releasing Harris, who scurried away to check his equipment. His gaze returned to Poppy as she stuffed the last of their emergency supplies into a pack. His darkness reached for her unconsciously, like water seeking its level. He had imagined staying, finding ways to shield them both from Milano's pursuit, using his shadow-walking abilities to keep them hidden while they built something that neither of their kinds could destroy.

But now that choice was dissolving like mist in sunlight.

They slipped from the cabin into pre-dawn darkness. Lunar extended his senses outward, detecting Milano's forces. There were three helicopter squadrons, ground vehicles on all major access roads, and energy scanners sweeping in grid patterns.

"This way," he directed, guiding them through a narrow ravine where he had detected a gap in Milano's surveillance net.

They moved in silence, Eclipse supported between Rowan and Poppy while Lunar flowed ahead and behind, sometimes splitting his essence to scout multiple routes simultaneously. The stars overhead began to fade as the first hint of dawn threatened the eastern horizon. Time slipped away with every step.

Lunar kept close to Poppy whenever possible, his darkness brushing against her arm, her shoulder, her cheek. Each contact sent ripples through his essence. Her warmth called to him with each step, making what he had to do infinitely harder.

He felt her glance at him repeatedly, questions in

her eyes that he could not answer. Not yet. Not until he was sure he had a plan.

The extraction point was a small clearing marked by crystalline rock formations that rose from the desert floor like frozen waterfalls. As Harris scurried about, setting up the dimensional array, Lunar felt the wrongness in the emerging energy patterns. The field fluctuated erratically. The devices emitted discordant frequencies instead of the harmonious resonance required.

"Coordinates match," Harris stated, his gaze moving over their environment. "Extraction window opens in seventeen Earth minutes. Give or take."

Eclipse moved with difficulty, still depleted. Rowan stayed close to him, her touch helping to steady him.

"So this is it," Rowan said softly. "Just wait for the spaceship and... what? They beam you up?"

Eclipse's confusion at the reference was evident in his energy patterns. Lunar recognized it from Poppy's cultural education attempts as they'd passed the hours in the cabin. The reference was to human entertainment about space travel. Some of it sounded ridiculous. He wasn't sure this planet would master the stars anytime soon. At least not in any meaningful way.

Lunar moved silently around the perimeter, his shadow essence extended to detect any approaching threats. He felt Poppy follow a few steps behind, her heartbeat elevated, her body temperature fluctuating with emotional turmoil.

"Milano is expanding their search grid. We have perhaps thirty minutes before they reach this sector," he reported, his voice deliberately neutral despite the chaos of calculations running through his consciousness.

He looked over the devices Harris had arranged. It was Zorveyan in origin. He doubted the trainee even knew what this technology was capable of.

The extraction field would create a dimensional fold, a temporary bridge between Earth and the waiting vessel. But without balanced energy signatures, that bridge would collapse, taking the ship with it. Whoever was riding it would be dispersed into the universe. If Eclipse and Lunar went without Solar's energy, there would be three-fourths darkness and not enough light. This was built to ensure they worked together if they were to leave. Only Solar was already in space.

Harris fidgeted nervously, checking and re-checking a small device. None of his motions was helpful. If anything, he was making the field worse.

"Thirteen minutes to the extraction window. All must be ready."

Lunar reached out with tendrils of his shadow essence, touching each device in sequence. He felt the energy matrix they were designed to generate and saw the instability in their configuration. Without Solar's light signature, and with Eclipse's twilight essence so severely compromised, the field would never stabilize.

Unless...

He withdrew his essence, condensing his form. There was another option. It could be calibrated for a single entity to go through. Eclipse alone would be a balance of light and dark. Or they could turn off the light energy, and Lunar could travel in darkness.

But that would mean...

"Lunar?" Poppy's voice broke through his calculations. She stood close now, her eyes searching his shadowed form. "What's wrong?"

He couldn't bring himself to answer directly. Instead, he moved toward Eclipse, who was conferring quietly with Rowan.

Luner approached the diplomat. "I require a moment of your attention, Eclipse."

Eclipse nodded, his twilight essence wavering slightly as he moved away from Rowan.

"I have completed an analysis of our mission parameters and outcomes," Lunar stated once they were out of human hearing range. "The experiment was designed to prove that opposing forces could coexist harmoniously when removed from their natural environment and given a common purpose."

"That is correct," Eclipse confirmed.

"By that metric, the mission has been successful. Solar and I maintained adequate cooperation. We each formed connections with Earth entities. We demonstrated adaptation to foreign environments." He paused, glancing at Poppy. "However, I have reached an unexpected conclusion. The connection formed with my Earth counterpart has created a harmonious resonance that exceeds mission parameters." He again paused, trying to find the right words. "What I mean to say is that I wish to remain on Earth."

Eclipse's twilight form stabilized momentarily as he processed Lunar's request.

Harris made a gurgling noise. "Not possible. Extraction coordinates programmed for three entities. Eclipse, Lunar, Harris."

Harris' biological makeup wouldn't be affected by the bridge, so he had nothing to worry about unless he were trapped on Earth.

"Then reprogram for two," Lunar replied coolly. "I have made my choice."

"The council will consider this abandonment of duty," Eclipse warned.

"Yes," Lunar agreed simply. He again looked at Poppy. She stared at him, her breathing coming in heavy gasps. "They will."

"They may declare you exiled permanently," Eclipse said.

"I am aware." Lunar would give up his home to be with her.

Poppy stepped closer to him. He felt her hope forming through their connection. "Are you sure about this? Your home—"

"Will never accept my true nature," Lunar interrupted. "Here, in darkness and in light, I am myself."

She reached to touch his face. He felt his energy automatically going toward her. "This is all I could ever want. I promise, we'll find a way to live where you'll be safe. Whatever it takes, as long as we're together."

The familiar threat of the helicopter sounded over the desert.

"Dammit. Why can't they just leave us alone?" Poppy frowned.

Lunar called out a warning to make sure Eclipse heard the threat.

Harris panicked even more. "Four minutes to extraction. Not enough time to relocate!"

"We need to mask our position," Poppy looked around helplessly. "We need something to slow them down."

Eclipse tried to expand his energy and instantly contracted back within himself. He was nowhere near optimal health. He could barely keep his energy together, let alone fight.

Lunar placed a hand on her arm to calm her. "I will create a diversion. My shadow-walking abilities allow me to move undetected."

"No," Poppy protested. "It's too dangerous."

"I am most suited to the task," Lunar insisted. "I have chosen this planet. I must begin defending it."

"Three minutes!" Harris cried.

The helicopter grew louder. Searchlights swept the distance.

As Lunar started to leave, Harris suddenly let out a distressed chirp, stopping him. The extraction devices flickered erratically.

"Problem. Big problem," Harris exclaimed. "Extraction field unstable. Energy matrix destabilizing!"

"What did you touch?" Lunar demanded. The configurations were worse than before. Whoever rode the bridge to the ship would be in for a painful journey.

Harris gestured helplessly.

"What's wrong?" Poppy asked.

Lunar felt his world crumbling. He wanted so badly to stay with her. To sweep her away into the night and never look back.

Eclipse attempted to expand his energy but immediately retracted in pain. His body temporarily dispersed before trying to regain cohesion.

"He can't do it," Lunar whispered.

"Let's run. All of us," Poppy said. "If it's not safe..."

"I'm sorry." Lunar touched her cheek.

"Lunar, wait—" Poppy began.

"Stop, you're not strong enough," Lunar ordered Eclipse, who was trying again to expand his energy. A look of understanding passed between them. They both understood the problem. "I can stabilize it with my shadow energy. I'll have to go up."

"But you wanted to stay," Eclipse said.

"As do you if given the choice," Lunar replied. He felt Eclipse's bond to Rowan. "But one of us must go. Your essence is too depleted for the journey. The council needs to know about Milano's technology."

"Can't Harris adjust it?" Poppy asked desperately.

Harris shook his head. "No. No. No."

"Lunar, please," Poppy begged. "We need more time."

Lunar led her away from the others. Her warmth reached for his darkness as it always had, the resonance between them vibrating at frequencies that defied measurement.

"One of us has to go. Eclipse is too weak." He stopped short of saying Harris had screwed up. "Without intervention, the field will create a microsingularity that will scatter them across dimensional planes."

"I don't know what that means," Poppy said.

"I must go," he said simply, his shadow essence reaching to brush her cheek.

"I know you think that," she whispered, tears tracking down her face.

"I think it because it must be," Lunar tried to explain.

A loud thud sounded behind him.

"Is he...?" Rowan began.

Harris was on the ground, holding his head. "Pudding."

"He's fine," Lunar dismissed.

Harris stood and stubbled in circles.

"If one of us doesn't control the energy, the ship will be lost," Lunar explained. "Solar, Dani, all those aboard, will die."

"Can't Harris...?" she tried to argue.

"A Galaxy Brides trainee cannot deliver critical intelligence," Lunar denied. "The council will dismiss him without verification from an authorized entity."

"Solar?"

"Someone needs to return with Solar. My people will not trust him if he's alone," Lunar persisted. "My presence will help balance his. We will both be needed if Eclipse is not there to represent neutrality."

Poppy's eyes filled with tears. Her mouth opened to argue, but no sound came out. He felt her pain like a physical blow, her energy signature spiking with distress. She wrapped her arms around him. He felt her tremble. "You're saying you have to go."

"Yes." He hated that he was the reason for the look of sadness on her face. He tried to find the words, but human language still did not have the capacity to explain all he felt.

"But you'll come back, right?" she whispered.

"The council will require detailed testimony. As

a Shadow Intelligence Specialist, my report carries authority."

"That's not an answer," Poppy insisted.

The helicopter sounds grew dangerously close, beating against the air like phaser blasts.

"I will return if possible," Lunar told Poppy. He didn't want to lie to her. But these emotions inside of him were not something he could put words to. Earth did not carry adequate phrases to make her understand. "Council protocols for intelligence matters are extensive."

"How long?" she asked, her words rushed as is she felt the seconds ticking away from them.

"Unknown."

Poppy's eyes glistened with tears, but her voice remained steady. "Then I'm coming with you."

"Not possible," Harris interjected. "Human physiology is not compatible with the extraction field. Would cause catastrophic molecular disruption!"

"He means you'd die," Lunar translated gently. "That I cannot allow."

"Fine," Poppy said to Lunar, her voice breaking. "Go and come back to me."

Lunar's shadow form condensed, becoming more defined as he made his decision.

"You have altered me in ways I cannot fully

calculate," Lunar said, allowing his essence to partially envelop her, one last embrace before separation. "The shadow territories taught that connection was weakness. You have shown me it is strength."

"Come back to me," she repeated, her hands passing through his darkness, creating ripples of sensation that would echo in his essence for eternity. "Promise me."

"Whatever it takes, I will return," he vowed, the words carrying the weight of an oath. What he didn't add was that if he did not return, it would be because he died trying, which was a real possibility with his people. "Whether in one Earth cycle or ten, I will find a way."

"Pudding!" Harris yelled, diving to the ground.

Eclipse again tried to expand his energy to help stabilize the devices but couldn't do it.

"Eclipse," Lunar admonished, "you must remain. Your twilight energy is too weak for the extraction. And Milano has already studied your energy patterns. They can't learn more from you that will harm our people. But if they were to find Solar or I..."

Eclipse's twilight energy pulsed with understanding, not needing him to finish stating the obvious. "If you go back, the council may not permit your return."

If it came to that, he wouldn't ask for permission.

"You have beaten Milano once," Lunar said. "You are best equipped to evade them."

"The threat must be communicated properly," Eclipse said. "The weapons they have developed, their knowledge of our physiology, and their intentions toward interstellar expansion. These represent a potential danger to Zorveya in the not so distant future."

Lunar moved closer to Eclipse. "Promise me you will protect Poppy until I return."

Eclipse's twilight essence pulsed weakly. "I promise. For as long as it takes."

"And tell her..." Lunar hesitated, his shadow patterns swirling chaotically as he tried to articulate what he had never been taught to express. There was so much he wanted to share with her. So much he wanted to explain. But he was out of time. "Tell her everything I could not."

Eclipse nodded.

Lunar pulled Poppy aside. "I must leave now."

She shook her head. The helicopter crested the ridge, drawing her gaze.

She grabbed onto him. "You come back to me."

He wanted to promise, but he the truth was his path was uncertain. "You are..."

Damn the human's for their lack of words. How could he say everything that was inside him?

"I..." Poppy looked helplessly at him.

They were out of time. He needed to leave.

"I wish there was more time," Lunar answered with one last caress against her body. He felt her shiver. The urge to sweep her into the night was almost too much to resist.

"Go." She nodded, though she tried to hold on to him as he stepped back.

Lunar's shadow essence contracted painfully. Turning to Eclipse, he said, "It has been educational serving with you, Diplomat Eclipse."

"And with you, Intelligence Specialist Lunar. Tell the council what happened here. Tell them Earth has potential beyond their imagining. And tell them I have found my true function at last."

Lunar nodded.

"Protect her," he told Eclipse, gesturing toward Poppy before he let his body shift into darkness to merge with the pre-dawn shadows.

Lunar flowed toward the extraction array, his shadow essence pouring into the devices. He forced himself to act. Leaving was the hardest thing he'd ever done.

The energy matrix responded to him, and the

discordant patterns harmonized. The dimensional bridge began to form, reality folding inward at the center of the array. His darkness pinpointed Solar's distant light waiting for him.

As Milano forces poured from vehicles at the clearing's edge, Lunar allowed himself one final look at Poppy. Her face was tear-streaked but determined, and her eyes fixed on his fading form. Her energy signature was already permanently etched into his essence.

The extraction field enveloped him completely, reality distorting painfully around his shadow form. As dimensions shifted and Earth fell away, Lunar held onto one thought with all his remaining consciousness.

He would return to her. Even if he had to tear through the fabric of reality itself. He would see Poppy again.

The extraction field collapsed, and darkness claimed him.

15

Darkness surrounded Lunar, but for the first time in his existence, he found no comfort in it.

The dimensional fold had torn him violently from Earth, his shadow essence compressed and stretched across the void before reforming aboard the Galaxy Brides vessel. That had been twenty-three Earth days ago. Twenty-three days of emptiness unlike anything he had experienced before.

He floated near the observation port, his form perfectly still as stars streaked past. Behind him, the ship hummed with activity. Bob and Gary chattered in their native tongue Dani and Solar engaged in what humans called relationship building. Lunar remained apart, as was his nature.

Yet solitude, once his preferred state, now felt hollow.

He did not want to be alone. In fact, it caused every speck of him to ache.

"You're doing that creepy statue thing again," Dani observed, appearing beside him with her characteristic human bluntness. "Solar says you haven't moved in six hours."

Lunar did not bother to correct her. It had been eight hours, seventeen minutes. "I am conserving energy."

"You're brooding," she countered. "And I get it. Really, I do."

He doubted that. How could she understand? She had Solar beside her. It had been her choice to accompany him rather than remain on Earth. She hadn't been forced to abandon the being who had fundamentally altered her existence.

"The Shadow Council will require detailed testimony regarding Milano's capabilities," he stated, deflecting from his emotional state. "I am organizing my observations."

A more accurate statement would be to say he was trying to piece together the mission logs he'd not finished on Earth.

Dani sighed. "For someone so smart, you can be really dense sometimes."

This assessment confused him. "I do not understand. My shadow essence is precisely calibrated for optimal perception."

"Exactly." She leaned against the viewport, forcing him to look at her. "You've barely spoken since we left Earth. Solar's worried about you, though he'd never say it. And I'm pretty sure you haven't processed a single emotion about leaving Poppy behind."

The name sent ripples through his essence, disturbing his carefully maintained composure. Poppy. Her warmth. Her perception. The way she had seen through his shadows from the very beginning. He felt an empty space where she belonged inside him.

"Processing emotions is not a shadow-dweller priority," he replied stiffly.

"And how's that working out for you?" Dani asked, her expression softening. "Because from where I'm standing, you're in pain. And you're not letting yourself feel it."

Pain. Yes, that was the correct designation. A constant, gnawing absence where Poppy's energy signature had resonated with his own. He had attempted to analyze this sensation using shadow intelligence protocols, categorizing and compartmentalizing. But the emptiness persisted, immune to his analytical approach.

"I failed her," he admitted finally, the words emerging before he could suppress them.

Dani's eyebrows rose in surprise at his candor. "What do you mean?"

"I had calculated seventeen different scenarios where both of us could have escaped Milano's pursuit. I had developed tactical approaches that would have allowed me to remain on Earth while still warning Zorveya of the threat. But the extraction field's instability was unforeseen."

"You didn't have a choice," Dani pointed out. "If you hadn't stabilized the field, we all would have been scattered across dimensions."

"There is always a choice," Lunar countered. "I failed to identify the correct variables in time."

The truth was more complex than he could articulate. For a shadow operative trained to analyze every possibility and predict all threats, he had been blindsided by the simple reality of the extraction field's energy requirements.

A novice error. An unforgivable oversight. A failure.

His failure.

"You know what your real problem is?" Dani asked, interrupting his spiral of self-recrimination.

"Please enlighten me," he replied, allowing a thread of sarcasm to enter his tone. It was a habit acquired from Poppy.

"You're mad at yourself because you didn't tell her you loved her."

The accusation struck with precision, sending shock waves through his shadow essence. His form wavered momentarily before he regained control.

"That terminology is imprecise," he managed.

Dani smiled sadly. "No, it's not. And you know it. You love her. You just didn't say it."

She was correct, of course. In those final moments before the extraction field had claimed him, he had spoken of altered states and resonance frequencies. He had used the clinical language of shadow intelligence rather than the simple Earth words that might have comforted her.

I love you.

Three syllables. So small, yet containing multitudes.

"I told her I would return," he said instead.

"That's something, at least." Dani pushed off from the viewport. "And we will go back. All of us. Just, you know, don't shut down until then, okay? Poppy wouldn't want that."

After she left, Lunar remained at the viewport, stars streaking past as the ship approached Zorveya. He allowed himself, just for a moment, to imagine what he should have said.

"I love you, Poppy Jensen. Not as a tactical advantage or a statistical anomaly, but simply, completely, as one being to another. I love your perception, your courage, your warmth. I love how you move through darkness without fear, how you reached for my shadows when others would have recoiled. I will return to you, not because duty demands it, but because existence without you is incomplete."

The words formed perfectly in his consciousness, where they could no longer reach her.

He should have said it. All of it.

Four more days passed before Zorveya appeared on the ship's sensors. The tidal-locked planet hung in space like a visual representation of conflict. One hemisphere blazed with eternal day, the other was shrouded in perpetual night, and between them was the narrow twilight band where Eclipse had lived.

"Home sweet home," Solar remarked as they prepared for planetary approach. His tone suggested the designation was as inaccurate for him as it now felt for Lunar.

"The council has acknowledged our arrival," Gary announced, checking the communication panel. "They have instructed us to proceed directly to the Shadow Chambers for debriefing."

"That is unexpected," Lunar observed. Protocol dictated initial processing through neutral Twilight Belt facilities.

"They are eager for your intelligence regarding Earth," Solar said. "The darkness will be unpleasant, but I did not protest the landing coordinates. I know you must be eager to finish your mission so we can return."

The gesture was not lost on Lunar.

"Perhaps," Lunar agreed.

As they descended through Zorveya's atmosphere toward the dark side of the planet, Lunar felt the familiar pull of his homeworld's energy patterns. The shadowed territory of Lunaris welcomed him. The perfect darkness a balm after the excessive light of Earth and the artificial illumination of the Galaxy Brides vessel.

Yet something had changed. Where once he had found the absolute darkness comforting, now it felt meaningless. Lacking the subtle variations of Earth's night, the interplay of moonlight and shadow that had created such complex patterns. Lacking Poppy's warmth to define its edges.

The landing platform extended from the Council Citadel, a massive structure built into the side of a mountain range that further shielded it from any stray light from the Twilight Belt. As they disembarked, Lunar noted the formal reception. Six council representatives waited with their shadow essences condensed into ceremonial configurations.

"Intelligence Specialist Lunar," the head councilor acknowledged. "Your return is noted with appropriate recognition."

The formal greeting followed shadow protocol perfectly, yet Lunar found himself craving the informal warmth of Earth greetings. A simple *"welcome home"* or even Poppy's casual *"hey you"* would have carried more genuine connection than this ritualized acknowledgment.

"Light-Dweller Solar and Earth-Entity Dani," the councilor continued, with noticeably less enthusiasm. "Your presence is accommodated."

Solar's light flared slightly at the dismissive tone. "We come bearing critical intelligence regarding threats to Zorveya's security."

Dani wore a tight space suit provided by Galaxy

Brides. It outlined her curves in a way that drew the attention of some of the council. They had visits from contained entities on the planet, but they were always a curiosity. Since the atmosphere was compatible with Earth, she didn't need a helmet to breathe.

"Yes," the councilor replied. "The council will hear this intelligence immediately."

They were escorted through the Citadel's winding corridors, deeper into the mountain where the darkness was absolute. Lunar moved with practiced ease, his shadow essence attuned to the subtle variations in pressure and temperature that guided navigation. Solar's light created an unwelcome glow around him, while Dani relied on that light to find her way through the darkness.

When they reached the council chamber, two guards stopped Dani from entering.

"It will be dark, but you will be safe," Solar told her. "I can feel you."

She frowned, but nodded.

The council chamber was designed to emphasize power disparities. The twelve council members occupied elevated positions around a circular depression where petitioners stood exposed from all sides. Lunar had been in this chamber three times before, each occasion related to intelligence mission assignments. Never had it felt so oppressive.

"Intelligence Specialist Lunar," the head councilor began once they were positioned in the center. "Your mission parameters were clear. You were to assess Earth's potential value or threat, determine if cross-zone cooperation was viable in an isolated environment, and report your findings. We have read your preliminary transmissions. Now we will hear your assessment."

Solar looked at him and his surprise hit Lunar like a wave.

"Yes. That was the outline to my," he gave a meaningful look at the head councilor, "*private* directives. Though I assume since you have revealed the plan in front of Solarestabinian of the Solarus Elite Guard, it no longer carries that designation, and I may speak freely."

The head councilor retracted a little at having been called out for his mistake.

Lunar didn't pause as he launched into his report. "Earth possesses technological development beyond previous estimates. While still primitive in many aspects, they have made significant advancements in energy manipulation, biological sciences, and communications."

"Summarize the Milano threat," another councilor demanded.

"Milano Enterprises is a human organization with access to technology derived from previous extraterrestrial encounters," Lunar explained. "They have developed weapons capable of disrupting Zorveyan energy patterns across all three signature types. They have detailed knowledge of our physiological vulnerabilities and apparent ambitions toward interstellar expansion. They are a faction and do not represent the whole of the human race."

The council members' shadow essences rippled with what might have been concern or anticipation. Lunar couldn't determine which, and the realization disturbed him. Before Earth, before Poppy, he would have read their reactions with perfect clarity.

"And the cooperation experiment?" the head councilor asked. "Did you and the light-dweller manage to coexist without conflict?"

Lunar glanced at Solar, who stood radiating with barely-contained impatience beside him.

"We did," Lunar confirmed. "Under Earth conditions, with shared objectives, cooperation was achievable. Furthermore, we both formed connections with Earth entities that facilitated a deeper understanding of the planet."

"Connections," a councilor repeated. The word carried unmistakable disapproval. "Yes. We have reviewed the preliminary reports from Galaxy Brides. You allowed emotional entanglements to compromise your judgment."

Lunar's shadow essence contracted defensively. "The connections formed were consistent with mission parameters."

"You chose to remain on Earth," another councilor stated accusingly. "You only returned because the extraction field required your energy signature. Your primary loyalty shifted from Lunaris to an Earth female."

Lunar frowned. Their alien hosts must have been watching them very closely. He hadn't discussed his desire to stay on Earth with their Galaxy Brides escorts. That meant Gary and Bob must have spied on them and reported everything.

The urge to throw Bob, Gary, and Harris into a blackhole was strong.

Lunar found he could no longer deny the truth of it. His connection to Poppy had indeed altered his priorities in ways that shadow protocol would consider compromising.

"My loyalty to Lunaris remains intact," he stated carefully. "However, my experience on Earth revealed possibilities beyond our traditional under-standing."

The council's collective disapproval manifested as a deepening of the chamber's darkness, a pressure that would have intimidated him before. Now, having experienced Poppy's acceptance of his true nature, their judgment seemed hollow.

"The Milano threat is real," Solar interjected, his light pulsing with barely contained frustration as he reacted to the shadows. "Their weapons could desta-bilize any Zorveyan who ventures to Earth. Their knowledge of our energy signatures suggests prepara-tion for potential conflict."

"And what would you suggest, light-dweller?" the head councilor asked, his shadow essence practically dripping with disdain.

Solar stood straighter, his golden form brighten-ing. "A joint mission. Representatives from all three zones, properly equipped and supported, to establish diplomatic relations with Earth while neutralizing the Milano threat. Our human contacts are willing to help us further integrate. Eclipse is already there."

"Bring Earth-Entity Dani," a member ordered. "Let us see these Earth creatures."

Dani was led into the chamber and instantly went toward Solar.

"Does she understand us?" the head councilor asked.

Dani touched beneath her ear where Galaxy Brides had implanted a translator. "Yes. I understand you."

"Have her turn around," one told Solar.

Dani crossed her arms over her chest and refused.

Several members allowed their shadow essences to reach for her. She gasped, swatting her hand through the air. Touching Solar's arm, she pulled on his energy. His light fed into her hand, giving her a threatening glow. The shadow essences automatically retreated.

Solar smirked.

The council members conferred among themselves in private communication. Lunar watched with growing unease.

"Your intelligence is valuable," the head councilor finally stated. "The council will determine appropriate responses to this Earth threat."

"Earth itself is not the threat," Lunar corrected, his essence pulsing with an emotion he would once have suppressed. "Milano represents a specific danger, but Earth contains potential allies. The connections we formed demonstrate compatibility previously thought impossible."

"You keep saying connections like this word means more than duty," a councilor said dismissively. "Your Earth female. The light-dweller's fire manipulator. Even the diplomat has apparently chosen exile for his human companion."

"They are not possessions," Lunar argued. "They are individuals with names. Eclipse studies Earth's knowledge systems with Rowan. Solar shares energy concepts with Dani. And Poppy—"

He faltered, his body rippling with the emotion he had been containing since he left her.

"Poppy understands darkness without fearing it," he continued, finding strength in speaking her name. "She perceives shadow frequencies no human should detect. She represents possibilities beyond our statistical models."

The council's disapproval intensified, but Lunar found he no longer cared. An Earth month of reflection had crystallized what he had been unable to articulate before extraction. His existence had fundamentally changed through knowing Poppy Jensen.

"You are obviously compromised," the head councilor stated flatly. "We can only assume your judgment is impaired by emotional contamination and alien light exposure."

"If understanding connection is contamination, then yes," Lunar agreed, automatically answering with his usual directness. "I am compromised. As is Solar. As is Eclipse, who chose to remain on Earth. Perhaps the real success of our mission was discovering what becomes possible when we move beyond isolation."

The council members' shadow essences contracted with shock at his insubordination. In Lunaris, such direct challenge to authority was unprecedented.

"Your mission reports will be analyzed," the head councilor stated after a moment of tense silence. "You are confined to the Citadel until further notice. The light-dweller and Earth female will be escorted to Twilight Belt diplomatic quarters."

As shadow guards materialized to escort them from the chamber, Lunar caught Solar's gaze. The light-dweller's golden form pulsed once in what Lunar recognized as silent agreement. They would not be separated so easily.

"Confined?" Lunar questioned. "On what grounds?"

"Potential psychological instability resulting from prolonged Earth exposure," came the cold reply. "Standard quarantine protocol. Three moon cycles in darkness should help realign your priorities."

Lunar's essence darkened with understanding. They had no intention of allowing him to return to Earth. The council had sent them on the mission expecting failure, and now that they had succeeded in unexpected ways, they were being detained.

"You will be contacted for further debriefing," the head councilor informed him as he was led away. "Your intelligence regarding Milano's capabilities is valuable, despite your compromised state."

Dani protested the ruling while Solar attempted to calm her. The guards maintained a careful distance from Solar's light, their shadow essences visibly uncomfortable with his radiance.

"This is bullshit," Dani hissed when Lunar approached, showing she had understood everything with her implanted translator. "They can't just lock you up because you fell in love."

The human terminology still felt imprecise to Lunar, yet he could no longer deny its fundamental accuracy. "They fear what they do not understand. Connection threatens their power structure."

"So what do we do?" Dani asked, looking between him and Solar.

Lunar's shadow essence rippled with newfound determination. "We adapt."

As they were separated, Lunar being led deeper into the shadow levels while Solar and Dani were escorted toward the Twilight Belt, he felt a strange calm settling over him. The council believed they could contain him through traditional means, shadow barriers, energy-dampening fields, and constant surveillance. They did not understand how Earth had changed him.

In his assigned chamber, a space designed for shadow-dwellers to regenerate in perfect darkness, Lunar allowed his essence to expand fully for the first time since leaving Earth. He reached outward, sensing the Citadel's security systems, the movement of guards, the energy patterns that regulated access to different levels.

And beneath it all, he felt a faint resonance, a distant warmth that he had carried with him across the stars. Poppy's energy signature, permanently etched into his own.

I will return to you, he promised silently. *Not as a shadow operative following mission parameters, but as Lunar, who loves Poppy Jensen with every particle of his existence.*

For the first time in his life, duty and desire aligned perfectly. And nothing in the universe would stop him from finding his way back to her.

16

Poppy awoke, reaching for something that wasn't there.

She'd done this every morning for thirty-seven days. Her hand stretched across the cot, fingers seeking the cool darkness that had once enveloped her while she slept. Each time, the empty space beside her felt like a physical blow.

Dawn light filtered through the cabin's heavy curtains. She kept them closed because brightness hurt in ways she couldn't explain. She preferred shadows now. They reminded her of him.

"You're up early," Rowan observed from the small kitchen table where she sat nursing a cup of coffee. Eclipse's twilight form hovered protectively beside her.

"Couldn't sleep," Poppy mumbled, though it was only partially true. She'd slept, but her dreams had been filled with Lunar. His star-patterned darkness had wrapped around her, and his cool touch had been a tease against her skin. Waking from those dreams was always worse than not sleeping at all.

"Eclipse made oatmeal," Rowan offered. "There's cinnamon."

Poppy nodded her thanks, though food held little appeal these days. She went through the motions anyway, spooning the warm cereal into a bowl and sitting across from them. Rowan and Eclipse exchanged one of those looks that said they were worried about her again.

"I'm fine," she said before they could start. "Just tired."

"You were working on the array until three," Eclipse noted, his twilight essence pulsing with what she'd learned was concern. "The transmission probability remains unchanged since yesterday."

The array. Her lifeline to sanity. A cobbled-together mess of salvaged electronics, modified radio equipment, and parts Eclipse had helped her design based on Zorveyan communication principles. For five weeks, she'd devoted every spare moment to building it, fine-tuning it, sending signals into the void.

"I modified the frequency modulator," she explained, stirring her oatmeal without eating it. "Thought maybe we were missing his bandwidth."

They didn't answer, which was answer enough. They thought she was wasting her time, that Lunar was gone forever, that the council would never let him return. They were too kind to say it directly, but she could see it in Rowan's sympathetic glances and Eclipse's careful explanations of Zorveyan politics.

"I'm going to check on the south perimeter," she announced, abandoning her breakfast. She couldn't bear their pity today.

Outside, the morning air held autumn's first bite. The forest surrounding their hidden cabin had begun its seasonal transformation, green giving way to gold and crimson. When they'd first arrived here, fleeing Milano's pursuit, the trees had been in full summer glory. Now they were preparing for winter.

How much time would pass before she saw him again? Would seasons change? Would she grow old waiting?

Poppy pushed the thought away. She wouldn't allow herself to think like that. Not today.

She walked the narrow trail that formed their

security perimeter, checking the simple alarm systems they'd rigged among the trees. Eclipse could sense approaching threats better than any technology, but they maintained the alarms as backup and to give Poppy something tactical to focus on.

A shadow moved differently from the others, drawing her attention to a clearing. For one heart-stopping moment, she thought—*hoped*—it was Lunar. But it was just a deer, browsing on fallen leaves before bounding away at her approach.

Her disappointment was a physical ache, a hollow feeling beneath her ribs that never quite went away. She'd tried to explain it to Rowan once, this constant sensation of missing something vital.

"It's like he took part of me with him," she'd said. "Like there's an actual piece missing."

Rowan had nodded, understanding in a way only someone who'd connected with a Zorveyan could. "Eclipse says they leave energy signatures on compatible beings. A kind of resonance."

Resonance. That was as good a word as any for this phantom connection, this sense that despite light years of separation, some thread still stretched between them.

Sometimes, in the deepest part of night when she worked on the array, she could almost feel Lunar's presence. It was a brief coolness against her skin, a shifting in the shadows that had nothing to do with Earth physics. In those moments, she would hold perfectly still, afraid that the slightest movement might break whatever fragile connection remained.

Poppy completed her circuit of the perimeter and headed back toward the cabin. The modified scanner she always carried detected no sign of Milano's specialized equipment. They'd been careful, changing locations twice before finding this abandoned ranger outpost. So far, it had remained secure.

Eclipse met her at the cabin door, his twilight form pulsing with what might have been excitement.

"Rowan has made contact with a journalist," he said without preamble. "Someone who might help expose Milano's operations."

Poppy nodded, processing this development. "Is it safe?"

"We are taking extensive precautions," Eclipse assured her. "Anonymous data drops, encrypted communications."

"Good." Exposing Milano had become their shared mission, something to focus on besides waiting and worrying. "I have some photos from the extraction site we could include. The weapons they were using weren't standard military issue."

Inside, Rowan was sorting through files, her reporter's training evident in her methodical approach. She looked up when Poppy entered, her expression softening.

"How's the perimeter?"

"Secure," Poppy reported, then hesitated. "I think I felt something again last night. Through the array. I think it was his energy calling out to me."

Rowan set down her files. "What kind of something?"

"A pattern in the static. Soft clicks." Poppy tried to keep the desperate hope from her voice. "It could have been interference, but..."

"I will examine the recording," Eclipse offered, his twilight essence rippling with encouragement.

"Thanks." Poppy managed a small smile. She appreciated that they never dismissed her hunches outright, even when they seemed far-fetched. "I'll be in my room for a bit."

Her room was barely more than a closet, but it had space for her cot and the small table that held her most precious possessions. There was a collection of shadow stones she'd gathered, similar to the ones she'd given Lunar. Next to those was a shirt she'd been wearing when he'd enveloped her in his essence, now folded carefully as if it might still contain traces of him. And, finally, a small notebook filled with calculations and frequency notations for the array.

Poppy sat on the edge of her cot, reaching for the largest of the shadow stones. Black tourmaline, cool and weighty in her palm. She closed her eyes, letting her consciousness drift the way she had when connecting with Lunar.

"Where are you?" she whispered to the emptiness. "Are you thinking of me?"

The stone remained inert, offering no answers. Yet sometimes, when she held it just right, she imagined she could feel a distant echo of his energy, a ghost of the connection they'd shared.

Was it real or just desperate wishful thinking? She couldn't tell anymore.

Hours passed as Poppy alternated between helping Rowan organize evidence against Milano and working on her array. The routine was familiar now. First, she'd check the frequencies, then adjust the calibration, send a signal pattern, listen for any response, and repeat. Logically, she knew the chances of reaching across light years with cobbled-together Earth technology were infinitesimal. But logic had little to do with why she kept trying.

As evening fell, Eclipse prepared dinner while

Rowan continued sorting through files. Their domesticity would have been comical under different circumstances, an alien diplomat cooking pasta while a fugitive journalist built a case against a shadowy corporation. Somehow, they'd found normalcy in their shared abnormal situation.

"You should eat something real," Rowan said when she caught Poppy grabbing an energy bar instead of joining them at the table. "Eclipse actually makes decent pasta now."

"Only minor molecular combustion occurred during preparation," Eclipse added in what Poppy recognized as his attempt at humor.

She smiled despite herself. "I'll eat. I just need to check one more frequency adjustment."

The array waited in what had once been a storage room, now transformed into her makeshift communications center. Solar panels on the cabin roof powered it, while a complex arrangement of antennas on the surrounding trees boosted its signal. Eclipse had helped with the design, incorporating elements of Zorveyan technology using Earth components.

Poppy adjusted the final dial and sent out the same signal she'd been transmitting for weeks. The pulses meant nothing to her, but Eclipse assured her Lunar would understand them.

Static answered her, as it always did. She was about to switch it off when something changed in the sound. There was a barely perceptible shift in the white noise, a patterned clicking where there should be none.

Her heart raced as she adjusted the reception frequency, trying to isolate the signal. For a moment, she thought she'd imagined it. Then it came again, clearer this time.

Three pulses. Pause. Three pulses.

"Eclipse," she yelled, her voice cracking with sudden emotion. "Eclipse, I need you!"

He appeared almost instantly, his twilight essence flowing through the doorway with liquid grace. "What is it?"

"Listen," she urged, adjusting the volume so the faint signal became audible.

Eclipse's form went absolutely still, his twilight essence contracting with what might have been shock. "That is a Zorveyan distress protocol."

"Is it—" Poppy couldn't finish the question, afraid of both possible answers.

"The energy signature is shadow-based," Eclipse confirmed, moving closer to the equipment. "It is similar to Lunar's pattern, though distorted by distance."

Poppy's legs gave out, and she sank onto the chair, her hands shaking. "He's alive. He's trying to reach us."

"It appears so," Eclipse agreed, his normally measured tone carrying a hint of excitement. "The transmission is coming from Zorveyan space, but it has been modified to penetrate Earth's atmosphere. Most interesting."

"Can we respond? Can we let him know we received it?"

Eclipse considered the array's capabilities, his essence pulsing as he calculated. "Perhaps. With modifications to boost the return signal."

Rowan appeared in the doorway, drawn by the commotion. "What's happening?"

"It's Lunar," Poppy said, unable to keep the tremor from her voice. "He's sending a signal."

The next hours passed in a blur of activity. Eclipse guided Poppy through modifications to the array while Rowan gathered additional power sources to boost their transmission. They worked with frantic purpose, afraid the faint connection might vanish as suddenly as it had appeared.

When they were ready, Poppy's hands hovered

over the transmitter, suddenly uncertain. What if it wasn't him? What if they were giving away their location to Milano or some other threat?

"The energy signature matches," Eclipse reassured her, sensing her hesitation. "And the transmission pattern is one only Lunar would know to use."

She nodded, took a deep breath, and sent their reply. It was the same pattern, followed by a series of pulses that Eclipse said would register as an Earth coordinate signature.

Then they waited.

Minutes stretched into an hour with no response. Poppy's initial elation began to fade into doubt. Had they imagined it? Had the connection been lost?

Just as she was about to give up, the static cleared for two seconds, and through the speakers came a single word, distorted but unmistakable:

"Coming."

Poppy stared at the array in shock, tears filling her eyes. "Did you hear that?"

Rowan squeezed her shoulder. "We heard it."

"He's coming back," Poppy whispered, as if saying it too loudly might make it untrue. "He's actually coming back."

Eclipse's twilight essence pulsed with cautious optimism. "It would appear so, though the logistics of such a journey are extraordinarily complex. The council would not easily permit his return."

"But he found a way," Poppy insisted, clinging to the single word like a lifeline. "He promised he would, and he found a way."

That night, Poppy lay on her cot staring at the ceiling, sleep impossible despite her exhaustion. One word played through her mind on endless repeat.

Coming.

She reached for the shadow stone beside her bed, clutching it to her chest. For the first time in thirty-seven days, the hollow feeling beneath her ribs had eased slightly. The missing piece hadn't returned, but now there was something else in its place.

Hope.

Outside her window, the night shadows seemed to pulse with new life, as if responding to her changed emotional state. Poppy watched them, imagining Lunar moving through them, his star patterns swirling as he found his way back to her across impossible distances.

"I'm waiting," she whispered to the darkness. "However long it takes, I'll be here."

The shadow stone in her hand seemed to grow warmer, though she knew it was probably just her own body heat. Still, she liked to imagine it was responding to her words, carrying them across the void to where Lunar might somehow hear them.

The missing piece of her remained missing, but now she understood. He hadn't taken it with him. He'd left it with her, a part of his essence embedded in hers, waiting to be made whole again when he returned.

Coming, the darkness seemed to whisper back. Coming home to you.

17

_____

THE COUNCIL'S CONTAINMENT MEASURES WERE
laughably inadequate.

Lunar moved through the shadow barriers as if
they were mist, his essence having evolved beyond
the simple constraints designed to hold traditional
shadow-dwellers. Four cycles of time had passed
since his confinement began, four cycles of
pretending compliance while secretly preparing for
escape. His only reprieve had been when they
brought him to the Twilight Belt to question him
with Dani and Solar.

He flowed through the final security checkpoint,
the guards oblivious to his passing. Earth had taught
him subtlety beyond what the people of Lunaris
could imagine. His essence had become something

new, not merely shadow, but the spaces between, the negative space that even darkness overlooked.

He moved through the shadows of the Citadel's lower levels, avoiding the few guards standing watch. Lunar had memorized the patrol patterns during his confinement, identifying the precise moment when security would be most vulnerable.

Solar waited at the predetermined location on the edge of the Twilight Belt, his golden form dimmed to avoid detection. Beside him stood Dani, tense with anticipation.

"You're late," Solar observed as Lunar materialized.

"The council added tertiary containment protocols," Lunar explained. "They're suspicious."

"With good reason," Dani muttered. "We're basically committing treason, right?"

Lunar's form rippled with amusement. "My people have no concept equivalent to treason. Only functionality or non-functionality. We will simply be classified as the latter."

"Great. Defective aliens. That's much better." Dani's sarcasm had become familiar during their shared confinement on Zorveya. It became quickly evident that she hadn't expected to be treated like a specimen during her time there, but that is exactly what happened. She'd spent most of her time locked indoors in the Twilight Belt.

"The transport is prepared?" Lunar asked Solar, ignoring her commentary.

Solar nodded. "Dani convinced Galaxy Brides to provide access. They are eager to avoid further complications with Earth operations. They have been surprisingly cooperative once Dani explained the alternatives."

"Threatened is more like it," Dani corrected with a smile that reminded Lunar of Poppy's determined expressions. "Turns out they're not exactly licensed to be dropping aliens on Earth. I suggested they might face consequences if certain regulations were enforced. I have no clue who those regulations are made by, but hey, it worked. I figured everyone has to answer to someone. I also had them send a message to Eclipse that we're coming home. I can't imagine how worried Poppy must be about you."

"You have my appreciation and I wish to hear more," Lunar acknowledged, "but we must depart immediately. The council has scheduled a special session regarding Earth containment protocols. Our absence will be discovered within six standard units."

The small transport vessel waited in an unused maintenance bay, its systems already primed for departure. Perhaps Bob and Gary possessed more intelligence than Lunar had initially calculated.

"We must leave the atmosphere before the orbital defense grid activates," Solar cautioned as they boarded. "The response to unauthorized departures is aggressive."

"Define aggressive," Dani said, strapping herself into one of the seats.

"Molecular dispersal," Solar replied, taking the pilot's position. His light-dweller training included flying.

"They'll shoot us down?" Dani's voice rose in alarm.

"Only after issuing three standardized warnings," Lunar assured her.

"Oh, well that's comforting," she drawled.

The transport's engines hummed to life. The sound immediately triggered alarm systems throughout the maintenance bay. Solar overrode the automated docking clamps that attempted to engage.

"Security response in four units," Lunar reported, monitoring the Citadel's communication channels.

The transport lurched forward, scraping against the bay doors as Solar forced them open. Alarms shrieked throughout the facility as they broke free of the Citadel's confines and accelerated into the night sky.

"We have company," Solar announced, the sensor display showing multiple pursuit craft launching behind them. "Defense grid activating."

Lunar extended his shadow essence into the ship's systems, diverting power from non-essential functions to the engines and shields. The vessel responded sluggishly, not designed for such maneuvers.

"I thought Galaxy Brides said this thing was fast," Dani shouted as the ship shuddered under Solar's evasive maneuvers.

"They are known to exaggerate certain performance metrics." Lunar checked the control panel.

"You mean they lie," Dani said.

"That would be accurate," Lunar agreed.

The pursuit crafts were gaining rapidly, their weapons systems charging as they closed the distance.

"They wouldn't really fire on us, would they?" Dani asked, knuckles white as she gripped her restraints. "I mean, Solar's practically royalty in the light zone. I'm pretty sure that's the only reason I wasn't put in a test tube."

"Former status is irrelevant to security protocols."

Solar pushed the transport to its limits as they climbed toward the upper atmosphere.

The first warning flickered across their communication system. *"Unauthorized departure detected. Return to designated coordinates immediately or face destruction."*

"First warning," Lunar noted unnecessarily.

The vessel shuddered as one of the pursuit craft managed a glancing shot against their shields. Systems flickered, the power fluctuating as the transport struggled to maintain integrity.

"Shields at sixty percent," Lunar reported. "Atmospheric boundary in fifteen."

The second warning came as they breached the upper cloud layers. The darkness of Lunaris gave way to the faint luminescence of Zorveya's upper atmosphere.

"This is your final warning," the automated system announced. *"Compliance is mandatory. Destruction protocols engaging in ten units."*

"What happened to three warnings?" Dani shouted.

Solar's form blazed with concentration, his golden light pulsing as he channeled energy directly into the ship's systems. The transport lurched forward with sudden acceleration, throwing them against their restraints.

"Five units to orbital boundary," Lunar counted down. "Four. Three."

The defense grid appeared on their sensors. It was a network of energy weapons positioned in geosynchronous orbit around the planet. Designed to prevent unauthorized entry, the weapons were equally effective at preventing escape.

"Two. One."

The grid activated, energy beams lancing toward their position with lethal precision. Solar banked sharply, the transport groaning under stresses it was never designed to endure. One beam grazed their port side, alarms blaring as systems began to fail.

"Hold on," Solar shouted, his essence flaring as he poured his own energy into the ship's failing shields.

Lunar did the same, extending his shadow essence to absorb and redirect the incoming energy. For a moment, he and Solar achieved a perfect balance of light and shadow, working in harmony to create a protective barrier around the vessel.

The moment stretched, time seeming to slow as they passed through the grid's final targeting zone. Then, suddenly, they were beyond it, the defense systems receding behind them as they broke free of Zorveya's orbit.

"We made it," Dani breathed, her face pale but determined. "We actually made it."

"The council will send pursuit vessels," Lunar cautioned, unwilling to celebrate prematurely. "And our transport has sustained significant damage."

"Can we reach Earth?" Dani asked.

Solar and Lunar exchanged glances, a silent calculation passing between them. Neither one of them bluntly answered her question, opting instead to shield her from the full gravity of their situation.

"The dimensional drive remains functional," Solar confirmed after checking the systems. "However, calibration will be difficult without optimal energy balance."

"Translation for the human?" Dani requested. "Don't sugarcoat it."

"The ship is equipped to handle a long distance jump. We can attempt to implement the dimensional fold to Earth," Lunar explained, "but it's dangerous without the coordinates to a safe landing zone. The trajectory calculation becomes imprecise. We need Eclipse to guide us to the right location."

"Imprecise," Dani repeated flatly. "As in, we might end up on the wrong planet?"

"As in we might end up scattered across multiple dimensional planes," Solar corrected. "Our energy signatures would be distributed across an infinite number of potential realities."

"Theoretically," Lunar added.

Dani closed her eyes briefly. "Of course. Because this wasn't terrifying enough already."

Suddenly, she reached into the bodice of her space suit. She pulled out a small object and handed it to Lunar. "Does this help? Gary said to give it to you once we were safe."

Lunar activated the small energy stone. It didn't have much data on it, but it did have the coordinates. Poppy had received Galaxy Brides' message. She was waiting. He felt his energy amplify. The resonance between them stretched across impossible distances, becoming his fixed point in the universe.

"I know we're not safe, but—" Dani said.

"It helps," Lunar interrupted. "We have a target."

Lunar moved to the navigation console, his shadow essence interfacing directly with the ship's dimensional calculator. "I can compensate for the missing twilight energy by modulating my shadow signature to approximate certain frequencies."

"That's not possible," Solar objected. "Shadow cannot mimic twilight."

"Not traditionally," Lunar agreed. "But Earth changed us both. My shadow essence has evolved beyond standard parameters."

To demonstrate, he allowed his form to shift, the darkness within him thinning slightly until hints of twilight-like energy became visible in his core. It wasn't true twilight, and Eclipse would have been insulted by the imitation, but it might be enough to balance the fold.

Solar's light dimmed slightly in what Lunar recognized as surprise. "When did you develop this capability?"

"During confinement," Lunar explained. "I had extensive time to experiment with the Earth modifications to my essence."

"Earth modifications," Dani repeated thoughtfully. "You mean Poppy."

Lunar didn't answer directly. "The calibration will require precise synchronization between our energy signatures. Even then, the success probability remains below optimal parameters."

"Again, translate that for the human. What are our chances?" Dani asked.

"Carrying a human with us? Thirty-seven percent," Lunar calculated.

"That's better than I expected," Solar admitted.

Dani looked between them. "You're both crazy, you know that? Thirty-seven percent is terrible odds."

"The alternative is returning to Zorveya or drifting through space, hoping we meet a friendly ship until our resources are depleted," Lunar pointed out.

"Neither one of you thought to mention this to me before we left the surface?" Dani asked.

Lunar and Solar shared a look.

"Right," Dani sighed. "Okay, then. Let's do it. Why not? We only live once. Might as well make it count."

They worked in silence, Lunar and Solar calibrating their energy signatures while the transport limped away from Zorveya. Long-range sensors showed pursuit vessels launching, but they remained hours behind. It was enough time to attempt the dimensional fold if they worked quickly.

As Lunar interfaced with the ship's systems, part of his consciousness remained fixed on that faint energy signature from Earth. Poppy.

"Calibration at eighty-four percent," he reported.

"It's not optimal, but it may be sufficient," Solar answered.

"Milano might be monitoring for arrivals," Lunar cautioned. "They tracked our original landing."

"That's probably because we crash landed in a public space," Solar countered.

"Can we mask our approach?" Dani asked.

"Plot a trajectory for Earth's moon," Solar instructed. "We can use it for gravitational assistance and to avoid detection."

Lunar considered the possibilities. "The damage to our vessel creates irregular energy patterns that might confuse standard detection protocols. If we time our arrival to coincide with a solar flare, the electromagnetic interference could provide additional concealment."

Solar checked the astronomical data. "The next significant solar activity occurs in two standard units. That gives us little margin for error."

"When has that ever stopped us?" Dani's attempt at humor didn't quite mask her anxiety, but Lunar appreciated the effort.

They completed the final preparations as the pursuit vessels closed the distance. The dimensional drive hummed with unstable energy. The balance between Solar's light and Lunar's shadow-twilight approximation created patterns that the ship's systems struggled to process.

"Dimensional fold initiating," Solar announced, his golden form pulsating as he channeled energy directly into the drive.

Lunar did the same, his new essence flowing into the systems, carefully modulated to fill the gaps where Eclipse's twilight energy should have been. The strain was immense, forcing him to draw on reserves he didn't know he possessed.

"Ten seconds," Solar counted. "Nine. Eight."

The pursuing vessels appeared on their long-range sensors, weapons charging.

"Seven. Six. Five."

Dani reached out, placing one hand on Solar's arm and the other on what passed for Lunar's shoulder, bridging them in a surprisingly effective way. Her hands trembled violently as her grip tightened. The calibration suddenly jumped to ninety-two percent.

"Four. Three."

"For Poppy," Dani said quietly to Lunar.

"Two. One."

Reality folded.

The sensation was unlike anything Lunar had experienced before. There was a reason ships didn't jump such great distances. This was chaotic, reality stretching and compressing around them as the imperfect energy balance struggled to stay on course.

Colors that shouldn't exist in deep space flashed through his consciousness. Sounds became visible. Light had weight, and darkness sang with voices that resembled Poppy's but weren't quite right. Lunar felt his shadow essence being pulled in multiple directions, fragments of his being threatening to scatter across dimensions.

With all his remaining strength, he forced himself to focus on the faint resonance of Poppy's energy signature.

For an eternity that might have been seconds or centuries, they existed in the space between realities. Then, with a violent surge of energy that nearly tore the transport apart, they emerged.

Alarms blared throughout the vessel. Systems failed in cascading sequences. Through the viewport, the familiar curve of Earth's moon filled their vision, its cratered surface rushing toward them at terminal velocity.

"Engines offline," Solar reported, his light dimmed from the effort of maintaining the fold. "Navigation compromised. Structural integrity failing."

"So in human terms," Dani translated, bracing herself, "we're going to crash."

"Impact in forty-seven seconds," Lunar confirmed, redirecting his remaining energy into the emergency systems.

"Can we make Earth's atmosphere?" Dani asked.

"No," Solar replied. "Our trajectory is locked on moon impact."

Lunar's shadow essence expanded throughout the ship, seeking any system that might still respond to his control. Most were beyond repair, but the emergency thrusters showed minimal functionality.

"I can adjust our impact vector," he announced. "Direct us toward a specific crater with optimal shadow conditions."

"Do it," Solar ordered, focusing his own energy on maintaining what little remained of their shields.

Lunar poured everything he had into the thrusters, ignoring the warnings of imminent system failure. The transport shuddered, veering slightly as its descent trajectory shifted toward a deep crater on the lunar surface.

"Secure yourselves," he ordered.

Dani tightened her restraints, her face set in determined lines. "If we survive this, I'm never leaving Earth again."

"Ten seconds," Lunar continued.

Solar's light flared brightly, surrounding Dani in a protective cocoon of golden energy. "I will absorb the impact force."

"Five seconds."

Lunar's thoughts turned to Poppy. So close now, yet still beyond reach. If they survived this impact, if he could reconstruct his essence in the lunar shadows, he might still find a way to reach her.

"Poppy," he whispered as the lunar surface rushed to meet them. "I'm coming."

The impact came with devastating force. The transport broke apart around them as they slammed into the crater floor. Lunar felt his shadow essence fragmenting, scattering across the impact zone despite his efforts to maintain cohesion.

Darkness claimed him. Not the comfortable darkness of Lunaris or the gentle night of Earth, but the absolute void of consciousness disrupted. His last awareness was of his essence spreading through the lunar shadows, seeking stability in the perfect darkness of the crater's depths.

Time lost meaning.

Then, gradually, awareness returned. Lunar found himself reforming in the deep shadow of the crater. Around him lay parts broken off the transport, twisted metal, and shattered components spread across the lunar surface. Their arrival had been far from subtle.

Solar was nearby, inside the bulk of the ship. Lunar automatically flowed toward the vessel, slipping through the cracks to get in. Dani was unconscious but alive within Solar's protective field.

"Status?" Lunar managed, his form still wavering as it reconsolidated.

"Functional. Oxygen is low. We must conserve it for Dani." Solar replied, though his light was dimmed significantly. "You appear severely fragmented."

"I will recover," Lunar assured him, though the process would take time that he was reluctant to spare.

"Can the ship reach Earth?" Solar asked the critical question. He focused all his strength on keeping Dani safe.

Lunar extended his senses, seeking any functional components among the wreckage. "The emergency beacon remains operational. If calibrated, we might establish communication with Eclipse."

"If we don't..." Solar looked at Dani. "She can't die like this."

"We won't let that happen," Lunar said, unsure how he was going to keep the promise.

Together, they tried to salvage what they could from the wreckage. Lunar's shadow essence flowed through broken systems while Solar used his light energy to power a makeshift communication device.

"The signal will be weak," Lunar cautioned. "And Milano may intercept it."

"We have no alternative," Solar pointed out.

Dani regained consciousness as they worked.

"Did we make it?" she asked groggily.

"We have reached Earth's moon," Solar informed her.

"The moon?" She leaned up in her chair to stare through a viewing port. Her breathing visibly deepened. Blood trickled from the back of her head. "Please tell me you have a plan."

Lunar calibrated the emergency beacon to match the frequency Galaxy Brides had given them. The connection was tenuous, the power barely sufficient to transmit across the distance to Earth. But it was their only hope.

He sent the simplest message possible, one that would require minimal power but convey everything necessary. "Help."

Then they waited, conserving their energy, hoping against probability that the message would reach its intended recipient. Lunar's fragmented essence continued to reconsolidate, drawing strength from the perfect darkness of the crater. Solar maintained an energy field around Dani to protect her from the lunar environment as oxygen reserves became dangerously low.

Dani wasn't doing well. Her body shook, and her eyelids drifted open and closed.

"No response," Solar observed as the makeshift beacon continued its silent transmission.

"The signal is weak," Lunar acknowledged. He felt his friend's worry over Dani.

After everything they had sacrificed to return, failure was unacceptable. Lunar moved closer to the beacon, allowing more of his shadow essence to flow into its systems, boosting its output.

"What are you doing?" Solar asked, noting the change in Lunar's energy pattern.

"Enhancing transmission power," Lunar explained. "My shadow essence can be converted to electromagnetic energy if properly modulated."

"That will delay your recovery," Solar warned.

"Acceptable cost," Lunar replied simply, glancing at Dani.

The memory of Poppy's face filled him. Just the thought of her could sustain him. He would drain his essence to nothing if it meant a chance at seeing her again.

The enhanced signal pulsed outward, crossing the distance to Earth in an instant. Lunar maintained the connection, his essence growing weaker as more energy transferred to the beacon.

"Conserve yourself," Solar demanded. "We may need your shadow-walking abilities to reach Earth if rescue doesn't come."

"Shadow-walking across such a vacuum would require more energy than I currently possess," Lunar admitted. "This is our optimal strategy."

Dani, who had been examining the lunar landscape through a viewport, suddenly pointed skyward. "Something's happening."

A distortion appeared in the space above their crater, a ripple in reality that reminded Lunar of the dimensional fold they had survived. But this was different, smaller, and more controlled.

"It's a targeted dimensional bridge," Solar observed, his light pulsing with surprise. "But who—"

The distortion stabilized, forming a small portal through which they could see Earth's blue atmosphere. A familiar voice crackled through their damaged communication system. "Lunar? Solar? Are you receiving this transmission?"

"Pudding?" Lunar identified. His essence rippled with what might have been relief, except for the fact Harris was not the hero he'd been hoping for.

"Dani is with us. Can you extract all of us?" Solar asked. He shared a worried look with Lunar.

"Yes?" Harris replied.

"This is not optimal," Lunar stated.

"We can't stay here," Dani whispered, reaching for Solar. She breathed heavily, as if her lungs struggled to pull in enough oxygen.

"Can you extract Dani safely?" Solar demanded.

"What are you doing on the moon? We sent you specific coordinates." Gary's voice replaced Harris'. "I want it on record that this is not our fault. You crashed that ship all on your own."

"Answer me," Solar yelled. "Or I swear I'll set fire to—"

"Your ship is damaged. The bridge is unstable," Gary rushed. "We can maintain it long enough for transit, but there's a significant risk of energy dispersal during the crossing."

"Meaning?" Dani prompted.

"Boom and poof," Harris answered. "Big mess."

"Your physical forms might not fully reconstitute on the other side," Gary clarified.

"Perfect," Dani muttered. Her head dipped forward, and she stopped talking.

"All must travel together if this is going to work," Bob said. "We need to act."

"What do you think? Do you have the reserves left to make it?" Solar asked, though they all knew there wasn't much of a choice.

Lunar gave another meaningful look to Dani. This was her best chance. She wouldn't survive much longer without air. If it were Poppy, he'd hope Solar would make the same sacrifice.

"I will attempt the crossing," he decided. "My essence is already fragmented. Further dispersal is an acceptable risk."

"Lunar—" Solar began.

"If I fail to reconstitute, tell Poppy," he paused. "Tell her... Tell her I kept my promise. I found a way back."

Before Solar could object further, Lunar gathered what remained of his shadow essence and faced the dimensional bridge. Solar lifted Dani into his arms. Lunar placed his hand on Dani's injured head. The contact helped stabilize their energies as they approached the portal's edge.

"Focus on Poppy's energy signature," Solar

advised. "The resonance between you will help guide us."

Lunar paused at the threshold, his fragmented form wavering between solidity and dispersion. Beyond the bridge lay Earth, Poppy, home as he now understood it. One final effort, one last risk, and he would reach her.

"For Poppy," he whispered, echoing Dani's earlier words.

They stepped into the dimensional bridge together.

Pain beyond description engulfed him as his already weakened body scattered further, pulled in countless directions by the unstable energies of the bridge. He felt himself fragmenting into shards that threatened to drift apart forever.

With what remained of his sanity, Lunar focused on the single constant that had guided him across the stars. Like a beacon in absolute darkness, Poppy called to him. She was his guide through the chaos.

Eclipse's twilight energy suddenly appeared in the void, reaching out to him, providing a structure around which his shadow could reform. But it wasn't enough.

Then, impossibly, he felt another energy joining Eclipse's efforts. This one was warmer and perfectly attuned to him. Poppy. Somehow, she reached for him through the dimensional bridge. With the help of Eclipse, her unique sensitivity to shadow frequencies allowed her to reconnect his scattered form.

"Come back to me," her voice whispered through the void, more feeling than sound. "I'm here. Follow my voice."

Lunar gathered the fragments of his consciousness, drawing them toward that beloved energy signature. Slowly, painfully, he began to reconsolidate, shadow particles coalescing around the framework of Eclipse's twilight and the warmth of Poppy's call.

With a final surge of effort that consumed his remaining strength, Lunar pushed through the dimensional barrier. Reality twisted around him one last time, then solidified as he fell through the portal onto solid ground.

Earth. He had made it.

His shadow essence was dangerously depleted, barely maintaining cohesion. Through fragmented awareness, he sensed Eclipse stabilizing him just as Lunar had done for Eclipse after Milano's attack. The dimensional bridge closed, and the landscape around them darkened.

"Dani? Solar?" he tried to ask.

"Lunar. Stay with me. Please stay with me." Gentle hands cradled what remained of his form.

Poppy.

The connection became stronger than ever now that distance no longer separated them. Her shadow sensitivity enveloped his fading essence, providing structure and stability where his own strength faltered.

"See there, Harris, I told you it would be fine," Gary's voice announced. "No human pudding. Put that bucket away."

"Poppy, I kept my promise," he managed through their connection. His consciousness flickered.

"You did," she agreed, tears in her voice. "Now keep another one. Stay with me."

"I should have told you I love you."

The last of his energy reserves were depleted. Lunar's consciousness faded into darkness. But this time, the darkness was not empty. It held Poppy's warmth, her light within shadow, guiding him back to himself.

His final thought, just before awareness faded, was simple and with perfect certainty. He had come home.

18

POPPY DIDN'T LEAVE LUNAR'S SIDE FOR THREE
days.

She sat cross-legged on the rocky ground beside
the makeshift recovery area Eclipse had created for
Lunar in the entrance of an old mine shaft. It wasn't
perfect, but it was darker than the ranger cabin and
quiet. There was just enough daylight for her to
move around without hurting herself.

She watched the star patterns slowly strengthen
within Lunar's body. Each tiny point of light was a
victory, a sign that he was recovering after his
journey through the void. A shadow crossed over the
entrance, drawing her attention away from the
hypnotic display.

"You should rest," Rowan said, quietly coming

inside. "Eclipse says he's stable now. You can't keep sleeping on this hard ground. Go back to the cabin. I'll stay with him."

"I'm not leaving him," Poppy replied, her voice hoarse from exhaustion. "Not when he crossed galaxies to come back to me. Not until I know he's all right."

Rowan didn't argue, just set down a mug of tea. "I'll come back in an hour to see if you want to wash up and stretch your legs."

"How's Dani?" Poppy asked.

"Better," Rowan answered. "Getting a little stir crazy. We're going to have to figure something out when everyone is well enough to travel. This cabin was not meant to hold six people indefinitely. Pete came by with more supplies. I hope you like canned peaches and warm beer. He said he had a lead on the next stop on the alien railroad. I think he meant camping in a literal abandoned train car in the mountains. But that's tomorrow's problem."

Rowan squeezed Poppy's shoulder before leaving the mine.

Poppy's fingers skidded over the dirty ground, feeling the subtle vibration of Lunar's growing energy.

"I know you can hear me," she whispered,

pressing her palm against his chest. "I can feel you getting stronger. Just keep fighting."

The moment Lunar fell through the dimensional bridge was the most terrifying experience of Poppy's life. She sensed him before she saw him, that familiar cool resonance that had haunted her since his departure. She instinctively reached out, but what returned wasn't entirely Lunar. It was a fragment of his scattered body, or at least, that's the only way she could describe it. She couldn't help but fear that part of him would forever remain out there, drifting in space for eternity.

"Dani didn't have much time left. He channeled most of his energy into the beacon to save her," Solar had explained. *"And he was already weak. By all calculations, he should not have survived the dimensional transit. The only sense I can make of it is your connection saved him."*

A subtle shift in the star patterns caught her attention. Poppy leaned closer, her breath fogging the chamber's surface as she watched a cluster of lights strengthen and multiply within Lunar's essence.

"That's it," she encouraged. "Come back to me."

The light shifted at the entrance, and Eclipse's twilight form flowed into the mine.

"There is improvement," he observed, his essence

extending to scan Lunar's condition. "His core patterns have stabilized, and peripheral reconsolidation is progressing at an increased rate."

He kept talking, going into detail about the process. Poppy rubbed the bridge of her nose.

"You know, you all talk like science professors," Poppy mumbled, too tired to decipher Eclipse's technical assessment. "That was not my best subject in school."

"He is healing," Eclipse clarified, his twilight essence pulsing with what she'd learned to recognize as gentle encouragement. "The resonance between you appears to be accelerating the process. Your presence helps."

"I'm not going anywhere," she assured him.

Eclipse lingered, his form shifting slightly in what she'd come to recognize as hesitation. "There is a matter of some urgency we must discuss. Regarding Milano."

Poppy glanced up, momentarily distracted from Lunar's recovery. "What now?"

"Solar has been monitoring their communications through equipment Galaxy Brides salvaged from their moon crash. Milano has detected the dimensional bridge activation. They are mobilizing search teams."

A chill ran through Poppy despite the warm day. "How close are they?"

"Not immediate, but concerning," Eclipse answered. "We should prepare contingency plans."

Poppy's gaze returned to Lunar's recovering form. "We can't move him. Not like this. Not while it's light out."

"I am aware," Eclipse said.

"We can take him deeper into the mine." Poppy started to stand. "Where it's darker."

"I regret the choice of this location, but it was the place that was close enough to hide him," Eclipse said. "It is as I said before. You cannot go deeper into the mine. It is not safe for your biology."

"Then what?" Her legs were stiff from sitting for so long.

"Rowan has made contact with her journalist colleague. The evidence package we compiled is being released to multiple news outlets within the hour. It may provide sufficient distraction to delay Milano's search efforts."

"And if it doesn't?"

Eclipse's twilight essence rippled in determination. "Then we defend this position. Solar and I have established perimeter countermeasures using modified Zorveyan technology."

Poppy nodded, grateful for Eclipse's calm competence and touched by the protectiveness all of them showed toward Lunar. "Thank you."

Eclipse hesitated again, then added, "There is one more thing. Bob and Gary sent a transmission from the council."

This caught Poppy's full attention. Milano and now Zorveyan threats? How many more storms were they expected to weather? Why couldn't everyone just leave them alone?

"What did they say?"

"They have officially classified Lunar as non-functional," Eclipse explained. "Essentially, exiled from Zorveya. Because of his high rank in the Solarus guard, Solar has been classified as being on a secret mission. They don't want to admit he chose to leave. I am on probation since they determined I was unable to return due to my condition. But there was an additional message, specifically for Lunar."

"What message?"

"The Shadow Intelligence Division acknowledged the value of his Milano threat assessment. They have agreed to establish a permanent observation post on Earth, with Lunar designated as the official liaison."

Poppy's heart skipped. "They're letting him stay? Officially?"

"It would appear so," Eclipse confirmed. "Though I suspect it is their way of saving face after failing to prevent him from leaving."

A soft laugh escaped her, the first genuine moment of joy since Lunar's arrival. "He outsmarted them even before he left. He knew they'd have to acknowledge his value eventually."

Eclipse's form brightened slightly. "Indeed."

"What about Solar?" Poppy asked, thinking of Dani. "Will they try to make him go back?"

"He's posted here with a similar arrangement through the light-dweller administration. It seems our connections with Earth have created an unexpected diplomatic channel."

After Eclipse departed, Poppy returned her attention to Lunar, a new hope warming her exhausted body. "Did you hear that? You have permission to stay. Not that you needed it, but still. No one will be hunting you from Zorveya."

Inside the chamber, the star patterns within Lunar's essence pulsed slightly brighter, as if responding to her words. Encouraged, Poppy continued speaking, telling him everything that had happened since he left—how she'd built the array, how Eclipse had taught her about Zorveyan energy patterns, how she'd felt him across the stars even when communication seemed impossible.

"I never stopped believing you'd come back," she whispered. "Even when everyone thought I was crazy for trying to reach you."

The star patterns shifted again, more dramatically this time. Poppy sat up straight, watching as Lunar's essence began to coalesce more rapidly, the scattered fragments of his shadow form drawing together into a more defined shape.

"Eclipse," she called, not taking her eyes off him. "Something's happening!"

Eclipse appeared immediately, his twilight essence flowing into the mine. Solar followed, his golden light dimmed to avoid disrupting the delicate balance of Lunar's recovery.

"His essence is reconsolidating at an accelerated rate," Eclipse confirmed. "The critical threshold has been reached."

"What does that mean?" Poppy demanded.

"It means," Solar explained, his tone carrying unusual warmth, "your love saved him."

The simple statement was strange coming from them.

The mine began to hum with increasing energy

as Lunar's essence continued to strengthen. Star patterns multiplied and brightened, swirling together into the familiar constellations Poppy had memorized during their time together. His form became more defined, edges solidifying from vapor into the humanoid shape she remembered.

"Step back," Eclipse ordered.

Poppy instantly stood and gave Lunar space.

Solar and Eclipse both began to glow, sending swirls of their energy toward their friend.

"Should I do something?" Her hands reached toward Lunar in hesitation.

"Not yet," Eclipse cautioned. "The process must complete naturally."

They watched as Lunar's essence continued its remarkable recovery. The star patterns within his darkness pulsed and swirled with increasing vigor, his form becoming more solid with each passing minute. Poppy never took her eyes off him, afraid that if she looked away even for a moment, he might fade again.

The subtle thrum of energy faded as the carefully maintained environment dissipated. For one terrifying moment, nothing happened. Then, slowly, Lunar's fully reconsolidated form drifted up from the ground.

"Poppy," he said, her name carrying all the emotion his shadow essence could express.

"Lunar," she whispered, tears filling her eyes as she reached for him.

His darkness enveloped her instantly, cool and familiar and perfect. The star patterns within his essence swirled rapidly where they touched her skin, creating those beautiful ripples of sensation she'd missed so desperately. The resonance between them, once stretched across impossible distances, now hummed with immediate connection.

Eclipse and Solar quietly withdrew, leaving them alone in their reunion.

"You came back." Poppy's hands passed through his darkness to find the more solid core beneath.

"I promised," Lunar replied, his form solidifying further at her touch. "Though the probability of success was significantly below optimal parameters."

Poppy laughed through her tears, the familiar clinical phrasing so perfectly Lunar that it made her heart ache with joy. "Just say it was nearly impossible and you did it anyway."

"Nearly impossible," he agreed, his essence rippling with what she recognized as his version of amusement. "Yet here I am."

"Here you are," she echoed, still not quite

believing it despite the solid evidence of his essence wrapped around her.

"Permanently," Lunar answered without hesitation.

"Forever," she agreed.

Lunar's essence shifted, forming a more solid manifestation of his humanoid shape. The star patterns within his darkness aligned into a configuration she'd never seen before, creating a symbol that glowed.

"On Zorveya, shadow-dwellers do not speak of emotional attachments," he said, his voice taking on a formal quality. "We communicate through energy patterns. This is the pattern of permanent connection, of chosen resonance."

Poppy traced the glowing symbol with her fingertips, feeling the energy respond to her touch. "It's beautiful. What does it mean, exactly?"

"In Earth terms," Lunar said, wrapping more tightly around her, "it means I love you, Poppy Jensen. Not as a tactical advantage or a statistical anomaly, but simply, completely, as one being to another. I love your perception, your courage, your warmth. I love how you move through darkness without fear, how you reached for my shadows when others would have recoiled."

The words she'd been waiting to hear, expressed with a poetry she hadn't known he possessed, brought fresh tears to her eyes. "I love you too. So much that I felt you across the stars. So much that I never stopped believing you'd find your way back."

Their energies merged in the perfect harmony they'd discovered in the desert nights so long ago, shadow and warmth creating something greater than either alone. This time, there was no fear of separation, no countdown to extraction, no Milano forces pursuing them. Just the promise of a future together.

"What happens now?" Poppy asked when they finally separated enough to speak again.

"Now," Lunar replied, "we adapt to new parameters. Together."

CHAPTER 19

EPILOGUE

THE MILANO STORY BROKE ACROSS ALL MAJOR news networks the following morning.

Poppy sat with the others in the cabin's main room, listening to an old radio as Rowan's journalist contact presented the evidence they'd compiled.

"Director Vega of Milano Enterprises declined to comment on these allegations," the journalist reported, "but sources within the government confirm that a joint task force has been assembled to investigate the company's activities."

"It worked," Dani said, grinning at Rowan. "Your media contacts came through."

"Thanks to the information Eclipse saw when he was at the facility," Rowan said.

"Milano's operational capacity will be significantly reduced while they defend against these allegations," Lunar observed, his form solid now as he sat beside Poppy, one shadow arm draped around her shoulders.

"They're not destroyed," Solar cautioned, his golden light pulsing with residual concern. "An organization with their resources will have contingency plans."

"True," Eclipse agreed, his twilight essence shifting thoughtfully. "But public exposure creates accountability they cannot easily circumvent. Their freedom to operate in shadows has been compromised."

"Speaking of operating in shadows," Poppy said, "has everyone decided what they're going to do when we leave here?"

The aliens exchanged glances, a silent communication passing between them.

"With Rowan's blessing, I will establish an observation post in the Northern twilight regions," Eclipse explained. "Monitoring Earth's development while providing cultural and scientific exchange opportunities when allies can be identified."

"With me as his human partner," Rowan added, linking her fingers with his twilight essence. "We're thinking of starting a research foundation. Something that bridges Earth and Zorveyan knowledge systems."

"Solar and I are heading to California," Dani announced. "Silicon Valley could use some extraterrestrial help, even if they don't know it, and I've got contacts in the tech world. No one is going to notice an alien in full makeup in the land of movies."

"We will introduce clean energy concepts that accelerate Earth's development while monitoring for Milano remnants," Solar elaborated, his golden form brightening with enthusiasm for the project.

All eyes turned to Lunar and Poppy.

"We're staying here," Poppy said simply. "The shadow territories need accurate intelligence about Earth, and I need to show Lunar more of those desert caves he liked so much."

"I will establish a shadow monitoring network," Lunar added. "Primarily focused on detecting any further extraterrestrial incursions similar to Milano's previous encounters."

"So we're splitting up?" Dani asked, a note of sadness in her voice.

"Establishing strategic observation points across multiple locations," Lunar corrected. "With regular convergence for information exchange."

"He means we'll all get together for holidays and

stuff," Poppy translated with a smile. "Different cities, same team."

"The Galaxy Alien Mail Order Brides experiment achieved unexpected success," Eclipse observed, his twilight essence pulsing with what might have been pride. "Three successful pairings across energy types."

"Bob and Gary should give you a refund for all the trouble," Dani muttered, though her smile belied the complaint.

"Speaking of Galaxy Brides," Solar said.

All three aliens turned to look at the cabin door.

"What is it?" Poppy asked.

She went to the window. Outside, Bob and Gary stood with Harris on the lawn.

Solar gestured for silence, and Eclipse cracked open the door.

"Let this be the final lesson as we complete your training," Gary said to Harris. "Every species needs different prodding to fall in love. It took us many cycles to perfect this process. Zorveyans need to feel like they're the smartest on the ship. So we distracted them with a spaceship that's falling apart, and gave you the faulty translator. Human biology needs to feel like it's life or death. We tried simulations, but they need the real deal, so you put them in danger."

Poppy frowned and glanced at the others.

"They did it on purpose?" Dani stiffened and balled her fists.

Eclipse opened the door all the way.

Harris looked over, startled.

"Don't worry, they don't speak our language," Bob said.

"But—" Harris began.

"Look how cute they are. Simple creatures." Bob laughed and slapped a hand against Gary's cheek. "Never knew what hit them. Though I'll admit that moon crash had me worried for a second. Especially after we lost that last couple in the active volcano."

"Another lesson," Gary told Harris. "Don't expect your subjects to follow simple directions. We gave them coordinates. They crashed on the moon instead."

"Can I throw them into a blackhole now?" Lunar asked.

"You almost killed us on purpose," Dani yelled.

She started to charge forward, but Solar grabbed hold of her. "Allow me."

Bob and Gary instantly looked horrified and lifted their hands in surprise.

"How...?" Bob asked.

"Gary said to take initiative. Since we were

coming to Earth, I calibrated the translators accordingly," Harris admitted.

Gary gave a nervous laugh. "Just having a little fun. Nothing to see here."

He took off running, waddling away as he left his friends behind. Bob gave chase.

Harris lifted his hand to wave. "Many blessings on your unions. I left you some extra equipment around back. Don't tell Bob."

Harris didn't run as he turned to follow his bosses.

"Bye, Pudding," Lunar said.

Later that night, Poppy and Lunar stood outside under the starlit sky. His shadow essence expanded in the darkness, finding comfort in the night while still maintaining contact with her. In the cabin behind them, their unlikely family of humans and aliens planned for a future none of them could have imagined before Galaxy Brides' experimental mission. Different paths but a shared purpose.

"Are you happy with our decision to live near the caves?" Lunar asked. "The desert is isolated from major population centers."

"It's perfect. Mapping the cave systems seems like a useful way to spend my time," Poppy assured him.

"I've always felt most at home in the dark. And now I know why. I was waiting for you to find me."

Lunar's essence rippled with pleasure at her words. "The statistical improbability of our meeting continues to fascinate me. The precise alignment of circumstances required—"

"Or maybe it was just meant to be," Poppy suggested, smiling at his analytical approach to what humans would call destiny.

"An imprecise concept," Lunar observed. "Yet I find I cannot entirely dismiss it."

Above them, stars filled the sky, countless points of light reflected in the darkness of Lunar's essence. Poppy leaned against him, feeling the cool resonance of his shadow energy harmonizing with her warmth. Different yet perfectly complementary, like the night and those who found beauty within it.

"The council believes my connection to you compromised my functionality," Lunar said softly. "They are incorrect. You have not weakened my shadow essence. You have expanded it. Given it purpose beyond calculation and analysis."

"And you've changed me too," Poppy replied. "I always sensed the shadows, but you taught me to truly understand them. To see the patterns within darkness that others miss."

Lunar's essence shifted, forming the symbol of permanent connection once more. It glowed against the night, a promise written in starlight. "On Zorveya, shadow-dwellers exist in isolation, even from each other. Here, with you, I have discovered what it means to be truly connected. To exist not just for function, but for something greater."

"Love," Poppy supplied, the simple Earth word that encompassed so much.

"Yes," Lunar agreed, no longer resisting the terminology. "Love."

Lunar enveloped her completely, star patterns swirling with emotion as he drew her close. "The statistical improbability of finding you across galaxies was incalculable. Yet here we are."

"Maybe some things can't be calculated," Poppy whispered. "Maybe some things just are."

"Perhaps," Lunar conceded. "I find I can accept that possibility. With you."

Above them, billions of stars shone against the perfect darkness of space. Below, their shadows merged into one.

Light and shadow. Forever connected.

Forever home.

The End

THE SERIES

Galaxy Alien Mail Order Brides Series

Spark

Flame

Blaze

Ice

Frost

Snow

Eclipse Bound

Solar Bound

Lunar Bound

KEEP READING!

DRAGON PRINCE

Qurilixen Lords Book One

Grier's fiery passion for Salena might be everything his dragon ever wanted but loving her might just lead to the destruction of everything he's trying to save.

WITH ALL THAT IS HAPPENING IN HIS LAND, THE upcoming shifter mating ceremony is the least of Grier's concerns. Even though he is heir prince of the dragonshifters, he doesn't have the authority needed to help the humans stranded in dragon territory, nor can he banish those who ruthlessly control them. Yet honor demands he finds an opportunity to intervene, and he hopes that doing so won't start a war the shifters can't win. Finding his destined mate couldn't have come at a worse time.

Salena knows what it is like to be a pawn of the Federation. They might have kidnapped her and brought her to this strange territory, but she will never do what they want of her... what everyone wants of her. The last thing the fugitive needs is the very public attention of a fierce dragon prince claiming they're fated by the gods—even if the sexy man makes her burn in more ways than one.

READING GUIDES

MICHELLE M. PILLOW NOVELS

Free Reading Guides

Download free reading guides at
MichellePillow.com.

ABOUT THE AUTHOR

New York Times & *USA TODAY*
Bestselling Author

Michelle loves to travel and try new things, whether it's a paranormal investigation of an old Vaudeville Theatre or climbing Mayan temples in Belize. She believes life is an adventure fueled by copious amounts of coffee.

Newly relocated to the American South, Michelle is involved in various film and documentary projects with her talented director husband. She is mom to a fantastic artist. And she's managed by a dog and cat who make sure she's meeting her deadlines.

For the most part she can be found wearing pajama pants and working in her office. There may or may not be dancing. It's all part of the creative process.

Come say hello! Michelle loves talking with readers on social media!

www.MichellePillow.com

facebook.com/AuthorMichellePillow

x.com/michellepillow

instagram.com/michellempillow

bookbub.com/authors/michelle-m-pillow

goodreads.com/Michelle_Pillow

amazon.com/author/michellepillow

youtube.com/michellepillow

pinterest.com/michellepillow

PILLOW FIGHTER FAN CLUB!

FAN OF MICHELLE M. PILLOW?

Want to join an awesome group of readers?
facebook.com/groups/MichellePillowFanClub

THANK YOU FOR READING!

Please Leave a Review

Please take a moment to share your thoughts by reviewing this book.

Be sure to check out Michelle's other titles at www.MichellePillow.com

Imprint

The Raven Books LLC
1723 University Ave Suite B #247
Oxford MS 38655
United States

Telephone Number: 1 (662) 484-4174
Email: theravenbooks@gmail.com
CEO: Michelle M. Pillow
Website: michellepillow.com

www.ingramcontent.com/pod-product-compliance
Lightning Source LLC
Chambersburg PA
CBHW071753110726
47908CB00006B/1794